# I, PETER RABBIT

ISBN

This edition published 2019

Published by HardtHouse
P.O Box 240 Buddina,
Queensland, Australia, 4557

www.hardthouse.com

A NOVEL BY
PAIGE BLOOMFIELD


*To My Beloved Family*

"I HAVE LEARNED NOW THAT WHILE THOSE
WHO SPEAK ABOUT ONE'S MISERIES USUALLY
HURT, THOSE WHO KEEP SILENCE HURT MORE."
C.S LEWIS

# PROLOGUE

It was unseasonably warm for the time of year, though being close to winter in Canada, it was still remarkably cool. The sun was high in the pristine, powder blue sky and the breeze rattled the few remaining leaves, which hung low from the branches above her head.

With only so many days left before she had to return to work, she had exactly seventy-two hours to make her decision.

Audrey shifted on her feet, uneasiness taking root in the pit of her stomach. It was only a few short weeks ago that she had been certain there was nothing that could or would ever change her mind. But now, everything was different.

Mulling over the changes that had taken place had occupied most of her morning. She had escaped the old cabin early, tip-toeing through the ancient halls, avoiding the creaking floorboards.

With old torn jeans tucked into thick soled boots that reached up to her knees, a striped jumper and a dark scarf loose around her neck, Audrey looked like the painter she was; creative and somewhat lost. Bohemian yet sophisticated.

Digging into her pocket, she pulled out the letter and scanned the pages again. It must have been the thirtieth time she had read the last letter she would ever receive from her father.

Somehow, in that moment, the words suddenly made sense.

Just as her mind formed around the cusp of an idea, the thick and pungent smell of smoke reached her nose.

Without a second thought, she ran for the cabin and the people she knew were inside.

# CHAPTER ONE

Peter Wood was sixty-four years old when his assistant found him on the lounge chair in his office with a glass of half finished, eighty year old brandy clasped between his frozen fingers. His head was slumped forward on his chest and his eyes were peacefully closed, his intention merely to sleep, when he was unexpectedly snatched from the land of the living.

In his other hand was a crumpled up piece of paper, filled with his sure, flowing script. Etched upon it was his last will and testament, deciding the destination of his considerable fortune, acquired from the business he had built from the ground up.

Harriet Bligh, Peter's assistant, let out an almighty scream when she touched a perfectly manicured hand to his stone cold cheek, believing a simple shake would awaken her slumbering employer. When her gesture failed, she stumbled backwards and tripped on a leather chair, withdrawn from its usual resting place under the conference table. Falling backwards into the bookshelf, she knocked what she knew to be a priceless moulded artwork onto the floor and heard it shatter against the polished wood.

Stricken with a sudden fear of being fired, she now looked to her boss's unseeing corpse with a small sense of gratitude, before humanity caught up to her. Running from the room, she dialled for an ambulance and proceeded to alert the entire floor of the morning's unwelcome and inexplicable event.

Over the course of the next few hours, an ambulance arrived

at the office building which loomed high above the city streets, Peter Wood's body was removed from the scene and his family were informed of his passing.

He would leave behind three children and a slew of ex-wives, the first of which was the only one with whom he ever considered the potency of his vows. Emily had kept the house outside of the city and ditched the last name when the divorce was finalised too many years ago to count.

Irreconcilable differences was the official reason for the termination of their marriage, but everyone in the immediate Wood family knew it was because Peter was more devoted to building his company than he was to building his marriage.

It was about the time that he made his first hundred million dollars, and added another fifteen hours to his already ridiculous working week, that Emily decided that she wanted to remember what it felt like to be appreciated by someone again. She wanted to be taken to dinner, to be told she was beautiful. Emily considered herself far too young to be wasting her years on a man who barely looked up when she entered a room.

Refusing any compensation other than the fully paid for home, situated an hour out of the city, Emily had filed for a divorce before the bubbles had fizzled out of Peter's celebratory champagne.

The very next day, Emily had moved Peter's belongings out of the two storey colonial home in which they had shared lives that had gradually become entirely separate. She had shifted everything into the top floor apartment in the city that kept a keen eye on the sprawling chaos of Toronto, putting him, consummately, in his place.

Since then, Peter had failed at four other marriages, the most recent of which was to Georgia Court, a thirty-nine year old blonde bombshell who made no attempt to pretend she had any higher ambitions than campaigning to make shopping a legitimate and respected career. Their divorce had been finalised three and a half months prior to his death, with a two hundred million dollar settlement.

The last Peter had heard of her, she was setting up a new home in Hollywood, with dreams of fame and enough fortune to make it happen. The twenty-six year old men's underwear model, with whom she had consistently cheated on Peter, was right by her side, riding the glory train into stardom.

Emily and Peter had been held together by their children. Mary, the eldest, was a high profile lawyer that earned more in an hour than most people did in a week. Her yearly income was seven figures. She was, to most, a cold-hearted woman, without the benefit of compassion. She maintained a rigorous routine, waking each morning at four thirty to run her five miles. She spent the rest of the day binging on health smoothies, slapping the pavement with her stilettos.

Second in line to the Wood's throne was Jamie; a man about town currently juggling a successful photography business and three girlfriends. Jamie Wood was to the modelling industry what Ansel Adams was to landscapes. He was scattered and artistic in a way that no one seemed to find endearing. What passed as creative genius was usually just intense moodiness.

Audrey was the youngest, and the black sheep of the family. As a painter, she adopted the idea that life was meant to be an adventure with more purpose than acquiring astronomical amounts of money. Refusing funds from her family, she afforded the rent by working in an art gallery, albeit a rather unsuccessful one. She was, as it so happened, the lifeblood of the gallery, and without her, it struggled to remain open.

Her small apartment, situated in the dodgy end of town, was a one bedroom studio with pale green paint peeling off the walls, revealing the dusty bricks behind. Mismatched furniture, salvaged mostly from garage sales and second hand stores, created an eclectic scene and there was the subtle smell of fresh rain and roses hanging in the air at all times, the source of which remained a mystery.

Audrey was bringing a portrait of the elderly woman, who lived next door, to life when her phone rang. Busy outlining the fourth wrinkle on the right cheek, which would soon enough be shrouded by a wispy cloud of smoke from the woman's cigarette, she nearly didn't answer when the shrill tone snapped her out of her reverie.

She sighed and pursed her lips at the unfinished picture. Nothing short of a perfectionist when it came to her artwork, she was never fully satisfied, though her skill could not be questioned. When she placed paintbrush to canvas, she rarely took a break. However, upon seeing her mother's name appear, she made an exception.

"Hello?" she spoke distractedly.

"Audrey," Emily's voice was quiet, hollow.

"What is it?" Audrey put down the paintbrush and stood up, immediately on edge.

"It's your father. He's... he's...dead."

Audrey remained motionless, her chest still with lack of

breathing.

"Audrey?"

"Are you at home?" she asked, now acutely aware she was breathless.

"Yes."

"I'll be right there."

Audrey threw her phone into her bag and ran out the door, locking it securely behind her. She had come home to a ransacked apartment three times before. She was considering acquiring a guard dog. Or at least a vaguely threatening sign.

Out on the steam filled street, with litter marking its territory at every corner and street urchins doing much the same, Audrey reached out a hand and flagged down a Taxi. Slipping into the backseat, she clasped a hand to her chest and tried to control her ragged breathing. She expected to be seeing all the wonderful moments that she had had with her father flicking like pages of a book in her mind's imagination, but there was nothing. She couldn't even conjure a picture of his smile. All she could think about was time. A fickle friend. A dangerous opponent and an advantageous ally.

She wished she had been more conscious of the time that was slipping through her fingers. Maybe then she would have made more of an effort, spent more days just sitting by her father's side.

Just when the guilt almost became too much to bear, Audrey remembered that she had given up trying to spend time with him for a very good reason. No matter how much time she made for her father, her father never made any time for her.

Audrey was the least successful of his three children, who

were each separated by three years. She had no interest in money, or a high paying career, and lacked any business sense that would lead him to groom her into his corporate kingdom. She was, she used to call herself, the Useless Daughter. She knew, deep down, her father's deficiency of interest in her stemmed from her lacking, which had become evident in her late teens.

The Taxi wound through the streets, and the scenery gradually transformed from the busy city to looming trees that stretched their limbs over the road, withered and bent like old men hunched in degradation. It was another twenty minutes before the Taxi pulled up at the end of the overstated driveway that eventually led to the home she had grown up in.

Audrey stood staring at the driveway, unmoving, long after the Taxi had disappeared. She knew what she would face in there. Pain. Loss. Devastation.

She was in on a secret shared only between herself and her mother. Despite the divorce and the long years of separation, Emily had never fallen out of love with Peter. Somewhere in the back of her mind she had always held a flicker of hope, as she watched him flit from woman to woman, that he would come back to her, promising he was going to change, and, this time, meaning it.

Audrey had even allowed herself to imagine that one day he would. They were two pieces of a puzzle; nothing and no one else ever fit quite right. It made sense for them to be together, but life has a strange way of convincing its victims to forsake even that which was practically written in stone.

One night, after downing a bottle of ninety-three year old wine, she declared her secret wish when she had divorced him.

Truthfully, she had said, she never expected him to allow the divorce, or, if he did, it would wake him enough that he would come crawling back to her, having returned to being the man she had fallen in love with. Emily had waited, single and stagnant, for two years after the divorce. When the second anniversary of signing the papers came around, she marked the occasion with a trip to Hawaii with her best friend, Bridget. There, she had, as she called it, rediscovered herself. She was still fun, still young, and still beautiful. She decided life wasn't so grim.

Taking a tentative step forward, Audrey forced herself to continue moving until she reached the stairs that led up to the front door of the pale blue house. With a deep and laboured breath, she ascended the stairs and let herself in.

Inside it was chaos. Mary, dressed in a figure hugging black suit that accentuated her flawless body, was shouting into her phone. She gave Audrey a half-hearted wave as she pointed a thin finger into the air to the chorus of a fleet of expletives. A dozen or so fellow lawyers, business partners and other suit-clad people walked around, each absorbed into the digital world found in their hands. Mary and Audrey had grown distant when Mary turned eighteen, leaving twelve year old Audrey to battle the tumultuous world of high school, boys and hormones, without guidance.

Audrey made her way through the gathering and into the open plan kitchen that lead out to the balcony, which was separated from the house by seven wood framed panels. Jamie stood at the open door, overlooking the rolling acreage. He looked like he was the lead singer of an indie rock band, with black skinny jeans, a baggy brown shirt and a dull, multi-coloured scarf wrapped around his neck. His shoulder length hair framed his face, and as Audrey stood by his side, she saw the flat, sad expression that he had adopted as his usual façade.

"Jamie," she breathed. "Are you alright?"

He shrugged, his eyes never straying from the furthest hill.

"Where is she?" Audrey asked.

Jamie simply pointed in front of him. Following his outstretched finger, Audrey walked outside and found her mother standing at the bottom of the stairs, wrapped in the only item of Peter's clothing that she had kept - a brown leather jacket that always smelled of his cologne, despite the fact that he hadn't worn it in years.

Seeing her standing there, searching the abyss for answers, Audrey realised her father was really gone. He was dead. She hadn't yet allowed her mind to properly register the inexplicable loss and what that would mean from here on. She had focused all of her energy on getting to her mother, and the hollow void was only just beginning to take root at the pit of her stomach.

She stifled a sob and felt hot tears sting her eyes. She suddenly felt as though someone was sitting on her chest, taking from her the chance to ever breathe again.

She walked silently until she stood beside her mother. Audrey couldn't speak a word. She only had a fervent wish for someone to be there for comfort. Someone strong, and warm, who didn't feel the same pain she felt, someone who could hold her and tell her...something, anything.

She realised that deep below the armoured surface of the human heart was the innate desire to be comforted in sorrows, whether they be great or small, insignificant or all consuming.

To be comforted was a reminder that one was worthy of love; somehow worth saving despite the fact that one often believes the sorrow was deserved, as were the consequences thereof. Or perhaps her mind was just being noisy once again, sprouting out thoughts over which she had no control.

Even standing amongst her family, Audrey felt alone; abandoned. As she always did. She shooed away the thought and wiped several tears that had made their way down her cheeks. The truth was that Audrey had been closer to Peter than Mary or Jamie. Until, of course, it had all ended.

Mary had been viciously jealous of the relationship and threw herself into her study and work in an effort to please him. Audrey knew that it had worked. The more successful she became, the less time Peter spent with Audrey. It had been the same with Jamie. As his career sky rocketed, and Audrey continued to produce a steady flow of unsold paintings, the favourites quickly became clear.

Standing there, she realised the person she wanted most to comfort her was the person she could never have. Her father.

She had a burning desire to feel his arms wrap around her shoulders and feel his lips press against her forehead. Something she hadn't experienced since she was sixteen. She wasn't ever going to see him again. The thoughts fell from her lips in a whisper, a voiceless cry. "When I wake up tomorrow, he will only be a memory."

Emily suddenly clasped her fingers to her lips and dropped to her knees. Her deep russet hair, flecked with silver, covered her face. Audrey lowered herself down and sat beside her.

She didn't extend a hand, or speak a word. She did the only

thing she could; she sat there and let her mother sob.

# CHAPTER TWO

Mary had to stop herself from throwing the phone across the room. Her father's lawyer was away on holiday in New Zealand and wasn't intending on returning for another seven weeks.

That, Mary had tried to explain over a crackling connection, simply wouldn't do. He would have to return early, and if need be Mary herself would cover the airfare.

"It's not about the money, Ms. Wood," Bradley Small retorted into the phone. "It's the principal. I simply cannot drop it all for each of my clients. If I did so, I would be chained to my desk."

Mary drew in a deep and steady breath and ended the call. She took a moment to steady herself, leaning her forehead against the wall. She didn't know what was wrong with her. Her mind was foggy. Normally there would be no way the obnoxious Mr. Small would ever emerge the winner of a verbal feud. Mary would wipe the floor with him. It was her job. It was what she did best. But today, there wasn't a single comeback she could think of. Her mind was an empty slate.

Clearing her throat, Mary shook her head. This was not her usual self, this shaky, pathetic wimp.

Straightening her black two thousand dollar suit jacket, she flicked her shoulder length jet black hair out of her face and waved a finger towards a skinny man, who wasn't two weeks out of law school. He was already regretting his choice to become an associate at Wood and Snow. "Langton," she snapped, "get me a coffee."

He looked confused, thinking about the distance between the house he stood in and the nearest coffee shop. "But the closest-"

"In the kitchen, you moron." Mary raised a finger to her temple, trying to cool herself. "Harrison, dig up everything, and I mean everything we have on Bradley Small. I want to know every dirty little secret he has, and then get him back on the phone."

The man named Harrison, with a clean-shaven face and slicked back hair, nodded, and turned to a computer, prepared to do what it took to please his employer of three years. The other lawyers that Mary had brought with her didn't allow themselves the small mercy of a break. Mary was known as a tyrant, who worked her employees like slaves and barely gave them a chance to catch their breath before throwing them into a new case.

Mary had always been proud of her strength. It was something she believed that her father had taught her. When she watched men cower underneath her, she felt somehow closer to him. There were, however, times when she wished someone would look at her like she was just a woman. Not that she would admit it.

Jamie walked up to her with two coffees in hand. He sipped one and passed her the other. "Your assistant is a moron."

"Yes," she sighed, "that's what I said."

"I caught him pouring half the packet of coffee into the plunger."

"You rescued it, didn't you?"

"Would I be drinking it if I hadn't?"

Mary sipped the brew and closed her eyes, a grateful smile

spreading across her face. Jamie had always been her favourite.

He was generous and kind, in a way that no one seemed to recognise properly or reward. When he was a child, he had looked up to Mary in the way he perhaps should have looked up to his mother.

During their teen years, they acted as a unit, forging their way through the tumultuous and exhausting years of puberty and education.

When Mary had graduated, Jamie was still in ninth. He was, for a full week, stricken at the idea of schooling without his sister. At Mary's prompting, he embedded himself into a club as a way to find his feet again. The Photography Club. Truthfully, Mary took at least a small amount of credit for Jamie's wildly successful career. It was she who pushed him into the club, where his peers had given helpful criticism on his photographs and projects.

"Ms. Wood?" Langton's voice tickled the back of Mary's neck. He had a habit of standing too close. She two took small steps backwards.

"What?" she snapped.

"There's a phone call for you."

"Mr. Small?" she asked.

"No, someone from the city morgue. He wants to speak to whoever is in charge of all this."

Mary snatched the receiver out of his hand and placed it to her ear, pierced with a long jewelled line. "This is Mary Wood."

"Ms. Wood, this is Norman Keller from the City Morgue. I was wondering when someone would be available to identify the body for our records."

"The body?" she hissed.

"Yes, the body of," he paused, as if checking his facts, "the body of Peter David Wood."

"My father, then," she snarled.

"Ah," he cleared his throat awkwardly. "Yes, your father. I am... I am very sorry for your loss."

"A little advice Mister, what was it?"

"Keller."

"Well, a little advice Mr Keller. Don't call the home of a grieving family on the day of their father's death to tell them to come look at a dead 'body'. Show a little decorum. I will be there in an hour." Mary's voice was hard, cold and bitter, like rough-edged steel. She handed the receiver back to Langton and looked across to Jamie, who shook his head and closed his eyes.

"The body?" he asked. "Really?"

"Don't even get me started."

Mary strode down the hall, Jamie following behind her, and searched for her mother until her eyes fell on her hunched frame, lingering underneath the suddenly deeply overcast sky.

She paused a moment at the glass doors, hesitation leaking into her bones. She didn't want to see the look on her face. It would be, she knew, the face of deep sorrow. Any emotion, particularly those of a negative nature, made Mary extremely uncomfortable. But as the eldest daughter, she knew she had a responsibility.

The small figure of Audrey, sitting beside her mother on the green grass, caused what was intended to be an internal sigh to catapult out of her mouth until her breath appeared as a white fog on the glass. Mary thought of Audrey as the family cat, which stumbled in and out of rooms and family functions, ragged and tattered. You loved her out of sentimentality and familial obligation rather than out of appreciation for her personality, which was, in her opinion, severely lacking.

She was ungrateful for what Mary had done for her, dissatisfied with her lot. Without Mary, Audrey would never have been able to pursue her artistic career. Mary steeled herself and smoothed the front of her already pristine suit. Pressing a hand to the door, she pushed it open and travelled down the steps.

"Audrey," she said in greeting.

Audrey turned and saw her sister towering above her, her red heels digging slightly into the grass. "Hi, Mary." She stood and wrapped her arms around her sister's waist, pressing her head against Mary's shoulder.

Mary felt Audrey shake with a small sob and, startled by the sudden embrace, could only bring herself to tap her gently on the back. "Quite the greeting," she said.

Audrey pulled back from the subtle rejection.

Mary tugged on the front of her jacket and cleared her throat. "I just received a phone call. We are needed at the city..." she paused as if considering a smoother way to deliver the term, but finding none, continued, "the city morgue. They need us to identify him."

Emily didn't speak a word. Instead, she rose to her feet slowly, lethargically, as if weighed down by years of regret and walked towards the house. She pressed her hand against Mary's shoulder and kissed her cheek as she passed.

Audrey lingered a little longer, the shock of Mary's words rattling her more fragile demeanour. She shivered involuntarily with the drop in temperature, caused by the incoming storm. The wind picked up slightly, brushing her thin brown hair around her face.

"Are you coming, then?" Mary asked.

Audrey met her eyes for a long moment. It was the first time she had seen in her six months. Their last meeting had been at Jamie's birthday dinner. Mary had called her an ignorant doormat and told her to get a real job.

Audrey had, she recalled, responded in kind.

"Yes, of course," Audrey said, quietly at first, before repeating herself in a volume that wouldn't be swept up by the braying wind.

As Mary turned away from her sister and escalated the stairs, Audrey closed her eyes, took a deep breath, and followed after her.

# CHAPTER THREE

The city morgue smelled like antibacterial soap and rust. At least, that was Audrey's opinion, as the pungent odour danced around on the tip of her nose.

Mr. Keller, expecting visitors, met them at his receptionist's desk and led them back into the morgue.

He was overly friendly, bustling around the four remaining members of the immediate Wood family. Mary had, it seemed, frightened the man, whose balding head beaded with sweat.

Inside, a number of metal doors were embedded into the walls. An avid fan of Castle, Audrey knew they were long fridges, containing the remaining shells of the departed.

Upon the far table, a figure lay motionless under a white sheet. Instinctively, Audrey knew it was her father who lay dormant and unbreathing there. She inhaled a sharp, bitter breath and froze in place.

The others continued on, traversing their way to the table. Mr. Keller stopped at the head of the body and pinched the corner of the sheet between his thumb and right index finger. "Are you coming, dear?" he asked, looking beyond the family towards Audrey.

Audrey took tentative steps forward until she reached the table upon which lay her father. With each member present and accounted for, Mr Keller looked to Emily. Though her dark hair was flecked with strands of silver, it held on to the depth of colour she had in her youth.

Mr Keller, who, despite what the deplorable phone call with

Mary suggested, was a compassionate and deep-thinking man, noticed a swell of tears fill Emily's pure blue eyes, turning them to glass.

"Are you ready?" he asked, leaning forward over the table just slightly, as if whispering a secret to her.

She nodded without looking up and meeting his eyes.

Slowly, he lifted the corner of the sheet and pulled it back until it sat smoothly, just above the line of his pectorals.

Audrey's breath was stolen from her lungs in a way that made her head start to spin. Her father's face seemed dull, colourless. His greying hair, trimmed short – as it always had been – caught the light from the fluorescent tubes hanging above him, making them appear whiter and shinier than they ever had. Beyond the lack of colour to his face, he looked just as he had the last time Audrey had seen him, so much so that she almost managed to convince herself that he was only sleeping on that cold metal bench. It was the stagnant smell in the air that refused to allow her refuge in the comforting thought.

It was the first time that Audrey had ever seen someone who was...dead. Her mind struggled to form the word, swirling it around inside her brain, until she felt as though she might vomit. There seemed to be such finality to it. His lying there, an incomplete life left abandoned, in a body that was unfeeling and empty.

Audrey stepped to the right until she stood alongside her mother and reached out a hand to her father. Her fingertips brushed his cheek, ever so lightly. She drew back her fingers with urgency. She knew that when someone died, their body went cold, but she was still, somehow, entirely unprepared to touch her father and not feel the warmth that used to flow from him. It was unnatural, disturbing. She waited with bated breath, her hand hovering somewhere in between a nightmare and reality. She could still feel the cold on her fingers; she rubbed them together as if trying to get it off.

Emily pressed a hand against the small of her back, a comforting gesture that reminded her that she was, in fact, not alone in the cold, stark room. She looked back at Mary, who stood very still, her face a mask that gave away nothing at all. Audrey did, however, wonder if, at that moment, Mary didn't seem to look a little older, a little wearier.

Jamie cleared his throat in an effort to retain the tears that threatened to escape his deep blue eyes.

He turned from the table and took the necessary steps to the door. He waited there, guarded.

Mr. Keller drew the sheet forward, ready to cover the face of the newest addition to his morgue. Emily raised a hand, blocking it. "Wait," she said, her voice raspy. "Just... wait."

"Of course." Mr. Keller dropped the sheet back in place and stepped back from the table. He turned and pretended to leaf through a folder.

Emily rested one hand on her ex-husband's chest and another on his forehead, seemingly unfazed by the temperature of his skin. Slowly she bent down, whispered something inaudible in his ear, and pressed her thin lips against his.

The gesture, small, yet somehow enormous, made Audrey's eyes burn. Her stomach lurched within her, protesting to the events of the day that had begun so ordinarily. She felt bile rise up the passageway of her throat, heading towards her mouth.

She swallowed and coughed, breaking the heavy silence.

As if in response, her mother pulled back from the body and nodded to Mr. Keller, who managed to look up from his papers in time to see. He hurriedly returned and pulled the sheet until Peter could be seen no more.

Audrey remained still as her mother headed to the door, followed closely by Mary. Staring at the sheet, she realised that that was the very last time she would ever see her father. She wished, suddenly, that she had paid closer attention, memorised every line of his face, done something other than stand there, blind, deaf and dumb to what was happening around her. Her eyes bored into the sheet as if trying to see through it to catch one last glimpse.

"Audrey." Emily's voice was firm with the strength of a woman, a mother, who had no other choice but to be the last remaining rock for her children.

With one last glance, Audrey turned away from the body that used to be her father, all the while trying to silence her racing mind.

# CHAPTER FOUR

Standing in front of the reception desk, the Wood family was silent; each member absorbed in the depth of their thoughts. Jamie sat in one of the three chairs that attempted to make the waiting room somewhat cosier. The fading wood frames and lumpy pillows were, sadly, not up to the task.

Mary waited, standing with all her weight pressed into the heels of her shoes. Her stick thin frame seemed hunched; weighed down.

Standing there was the first time that Audrey noticed the music playing softly in the background.

Classical. Maybe Beethoven. It gave her the feeling of being in an elevator.

"Are there any forms we need to fill out, Mr. Keller?" Emily asked, wrapping her arms around her waist.

"Yes, these." He lifted the forms onto the rim of the bench and handed her a pen. "Also, there were some personal effects on the...your, uh, Mr. Wood. I have them here if you would like to collect them. One of the items appears to be his Will."

"I'm sorry?" Emily was confused. "Peter's Will? I would have thought it would be with his lawyer."

"Well, this was on his person. Handwritten. Here." Mr. Keller handed over a medium-sized brown paper bag. "You can empty the contents on that table, just over there, if you would like."

Emily quickly leafed through the papers, signed where required, and took the bag. Followed by her three children, she stopped at the table in the corner of the room and removed the items from the bag.

She placed the gold pen, engraved with his name, which she had given him, beside his neatly folded clothes. Together with his wallet, silver pocket watch and thin-framed glasses, the crumpled piece of paper made up the contents of the bag. Audrey leaned around Mary to watch as Emily unfolded the paper. Her eyes scanned her father's elegant script, but she couldn't make sense of the words.

"Read it aloud to me," Mary instructed, all lawyer now.

Emily began in a puzzled tone, "I, Peter Rabbit, do hereby bequeath my earthly fortune to..."

Mary snatched the paper out of her mother's hand. "To whom?" she demanded from the paper, shaking it slightly in her hands. "I have to make a call."

"What does it mean?" Audrey asked, stepping back from Mary as she turned violently and exited the room.

"Who is Peter Rabbit?" Jamie asked. "I mean...is he talking about the Peter Rabbit. From the books?"

Emily raised a hand and pressed her palm against her forehead. "I have absolutely no idea."

# CHAPTER FIVE

They each were perched in their individual chairs, sitting in front of the looming desk that belonged to Mary Wood. Her office was stark and cold, professional and uninviting. The only decorations were her awards that hung in giant, over-compensating frames, and a single, small painting Audrey had created for her when she had opened the doors to her company for the very first time.

Emily sat still on the high-backed Victorian style chair, her eyes directed squarely at a small spot on the carpet. Jamie was sitting cross-legged on the two seater sofa, as Audrey stood up and walked to the window.

"How long is she going to keep us waiting?" Audrey finally asked, fracturing the stagnant silence.

"She's busy," Jamie announced, ever the supporter of his sister. "She has important things to do." Jamie and Mary had always had a secret world that Audrey had never been invited to join. Most days, she was fine with that, but on others, its bitter sting was unbearable.

At that moment, the doors opened, and Mary walked into the room. "Sorry to keep you all waiting." She sounded aloof, as though she were speaking to clients she barely knew, not her own family. "I had to deal with some things." She sat down behind her desk.

"Mary," Emily began, looking up from the carpet, "do you have any answers?"

"Yes, I do. The will we found has no legal bearing, obviously. It doesn't say his real name, and it doesn't mention who he leaves his belongings to."

Mary paused. Everyone waited silently for her to continue.

"The problem remaining, is that I have spoken to Dad's lawyer, and he has no record of any Will. Only a letter, and some strict instructions. This is why I should have been his lawyer. He is so stubborn." Mary pursed her lips. "*Was*."

"What did the letter say?" Jamie asked.

"I have it here," Mary said. "I had it emailed to me. One of Mr. Small's receptionists at Dad's law firm became more than helpful after I went down there for a little visit."

"Read it to me, sweetheart," Emily said. Her voice was soft, decayed. She sat further back in the chair and folded her right leg over her left.

"Of course," Mary replied. A few clicks of her mouse later, and the email appeared on her screen. She cleared her throat and began,

*"To my family,*

*I've let you down. All of you. There's nothing I can say that will change, or fix anything, but I cannot rest until I have said, at the very least, that I'm sorry.*

*Jamie – my son. I never thought I would be the kind of father who was too afraid to tell his son that he loves him. But, upon reflection of the past twenty-six years, I've realised that that is exactly who I am. I'm sorry – I should have told you every day that you make me so proud, and I love you.*

*Mary – my first. When I first held you in my arms, I couldn't believe that I had been so naïve. Before you, I thought I was whole. But it wasn't until you looked up at me with your beautiful brown eyes, that*

came straight from me, that I realised that you filled a hole that I didn't even know I had. And I loved you more than I ever thought possible. To me, you are perfect, lovely beyond words. Remember that you don't always have to be so strong. Your fragility, which you try so hard to mask, is indescribably beautiful.

Audrey – my Mona Lisa. You have always been able to surprise me. Your talent is extraordinary, and I know that I never told you that. I have never met someone with so much heart, so much compassion. It moves me to know that someone like you loves me, and stands by me despite my downfalls as a father. I know you have always felt as though you don't belong, and that, in so many ways, is my fault. But if I can do one thing for you, it is to remind you that you do belong. You are my daughter, a part of me. Your extraordinary beauty, which radiates from deep within you, is a beacon of hope to me. I love you.

Emily – the love of my life. I am such a fool. It is a burden I carry daily to know that I allowed you to believe that, for even one second, money or this business were more important than you. My priorities have been flawed, beyond words. I let you walk away, and I didn't fight for you. Since then, I've buriedmyself in empty relationships, trying to find pieces of you in strangers. The word sorry falls pitifully short, but it is the only word I have – I'm so deeply, truly sorry. I just want you to know that I never stopped loving you. Not one day has passed where I haven't mourned the loss of our relationship, the end of our marriage. You are the sun and the moon, and every star in the sky to me, and I have never loved another. You have my heart. Then, now and always. I love you.

I have allowed this family to fall apart. For my final act, the end scene, I'm going to put you back together again. It's time you learned my story, the story of the boy called Peter Rabbit. With this letter, *there are guidelines you must all follow, to the letter, in order to gain access to my Will. Your deadline is three weeks from the date of my death. If you have not retrieved the Will by then, my lawyer is under instructions to dismantle Wood Incorporated, piece by piece, until nothing at all remains.*

*I love you. Each and every one of you. Peter."*

Mary finished reading the letter, silent tears drawing a line through her makeup. She cleared her throat and brushed away the droplets trailing down her cheeks. "The instructions are with the email. The first is to go to Canim Lake, where his family still has acreage."

The room was silent for a number of minutes, heavy with clouded thoughts and running emotions. Audrey was the first to speak. "So, we fly from Toronto to British Columbia?"

"No," Mary replied.

"We drive?" Audrey asked, confused.

"It's over 4,000 kilometres away!" Jamie threw his hands in the air. "I have to work."

"We all have to work, Jamie," Mary smoothly reminded him. "But, no. The instructions are that we do both. We drive from here to Tenner Airfield, then fly the rest of the way."

"Where's that?" Jamie asked. "I've never heard of it."

"It's a thousand kilometres away."

"How do you feel about this?" Audrey placed a hand on Emily's knee. "Are you all right?"

Emily's face was red from shed tears. Audrey could see her chest rise and fall with rapid, sharp breaths. "I think," she began, swallowing hard, "we go home and pack. We leave tomorrow morning, at five."

Audrey stood in front of her open closet, holding her breath until her cheeks puffed out, like she used to do when she was little. Her closet, usually sparse and underwhelming, seemed overbearing, like sweaters and sweat pants were going to leap down and swallow her whole. She had just gotten off the phone with the gallery, informing them she needed a few weeks off work due to the sudden death of her father. Dmitri and Lisa were more than accommodating. She had worked for the husband and wife duo for three years now, and this was the first time she had ever asked for time off. They felt they owed it to her. Without meaning to, however, Lisa swept in a guilt-ridden comment, declaring they were probably going to default on the rent until she returned. Lisa had never been the compassionate one.

Audrey had hung up the phone and thrown it, aggressively, onto her bed. She had wanted to aim at the wall and see the phone shatter into a million pieces, to satisfy her more dramatic side, but she knew she couldn't afford a new one. Audrey walked towards the hanging clothes and leaned forward until her forehead pressed against the back wall, and she was enveloped in clothes.

There, drowning in darkness and cotton, she felt a stillness rest down upon her shoulders. For a brief moment, she felt at peace in the silence. But the peace was quickly and violently replaced by intense sorrow. Her eyes brimmed with tears, and as she squeezed them closed, fat, salty droplets trickled down her face. The tears continued until she could no longer restrain the emotion that reached up from the pit of her stomach and slammed a hand around her throat, strangling her. She started to rake in short, harsh breaths, to combat ragged sobs that had breached the surface and shattered the façade of her composure, like a bullet to glass.

Her knees buckled beneath her until she landed solidly on the floor. Surrendering, she gave in and curled up amongst her shoes, sobbing, deep into the night.

Audrey's head snapped up and slammed against a brick wall with the sound of the jangle of her phone.

"What the-?" she muttered, raising a hand to the back of her head, where a growing lump began to protrude. She looked around, eyeing the shoes and clothes dangling against her face and sighed.

Pulling herself out of the cupboard, she reached for her phone just in time. "Hello?" she murmured.

"Audrey?"

"Mom?"

"Honey, where are you? It's five o'clock. We're all waiting for you."

"What?" She stood up and sighed as she noticed her empty suitcase. "I'm sorry, I fell asleep in the cupboard."

"What?" Emily asked. "The cupboard? I don't understand."

"I'm coming. Now. I'll be there. Just..." Hanging up the phone, Audrey threw her clothes into her suitcase; a random selection of whatever she could quickly get her hands on. Zipping it shut, she whipped off her clothes and dunked herself in the shower, before dressing haphazardly and running out the door.

# CHAPTER SIX

Emily stood by the Audi Q7, lingering near the driver's side, while the large willow trees swayed in the gentle breeze overhead. She could just about tune out the sound of Mary and Jamie's moaning at Audrey's tardiness, basking as she was in the early rays of the cool autumn sun.

She couldn't get her first semester at college out of her mind. It was a raining afternoon, the perfect scene set for her emotional turmoil. Emily had just found out her Grandmother, the woman who had raised her, was dead. She had åjust moved out of home, into a dorm that felt as though it were a million miles away from anything familiar, and her hometown boyfriend had written to tell her he was seeing someone else.

It was the first time she had felt truly and irrevocably alone. Being young and cloaked in the purity of innocence, having yet to experience the bitterness life could bring, Emily was distraught at her first real taste of sadness and sorrow. She was sure that nothing good could ever come from life. She saw her days flash forward in front of her, an acrimonious swirling whirlwind of chaos that could never provide her with love or laughter.

She had met Peter the next day, and he spent the week trying to prove her wrong.

Now, all those years later, a world without Peter seemed too strange and unfamiliar. She felt that sting of loneliness again, intensified so deeply she thought her heart might explode within her.

"I'm so sorry, Mom."

Emily spun to see Audrey standing beside her, looking weary. She smiled warmly at her daughter and pressed a hand to her cheek. "Let's go."

It wasn't until they had travelled for an hour and a half that Mary and Jamie finally let it rest that Audrey was an hour late, and how this reflected on her personal issues with Peter, issues that Mary and Jamie denied having of their own.

Mary, being the lawyer, took the lead in the case of the Sibling's versus the Black Sheep, letting Jamie just pipe up every now and then with a comment of his own.

Emily did her best to diffuse the comments softly, but not even she had mastered the ability to stop Mary from speaking her mind.

"All I'm saying," Mary had said, "is that if you really cared about this trip, and by extension, our father, then you would have been here on time, instead of swanning about in your apartment, painting cats, dogs and neighbours in your underwear."

Audrey had never painted in her underwear before, nor painted a dog or cat, so the comment seemed far and away out of line. "And all I'm saying, Mary, is that for those of us within the human race, you know, people with a soul, we tend to make mistakes. Little ones, big ones, ones that matter and ones that don't. It's not customary to lay them out like a lamb for the slaughter for it." She twisted her body from the front seat to better see Mary and Jamie, who sat in the back, looking like a posse being chauffeured.

"Mary, let it go. It doesn't matter." Emily gripped the steering wheel a little tighter, until her knuckles became white.

"It does matter," Jamie added. "I had to call the airfield and postpone our flight. It cost us four hundred dollars. Imagine if we were flying commercial. We would have to wait until tomorrow."

"Oh, four hundred dollars. Thirty minutes work for Mary. My goodness," Audrey said spitefully. "What a terrible shame."

"You're exactly right, Audrey. How long would it take you to earn that much money, hmm?"

"That's it!" Emily violently pulled the car off the road, to the chorus of beeping horns. She slammed the brakes on, parked precariously on the side strip, unbuckled and turned around in her seat to face her children. "If I hear so much as one more word about this from any of you, so help me, I will kick you out of this car and you will find your own way to Canim Lake, is that understood?"

Since the soft touch hadn't worked, Emily pulled out the 'Mother Treatment' which she hadn't used since Audrey was in her final year of high school. Her children looked back at her in stunned silence.

"Do you know what this is about? What we're doing here? Your father is dead. Dead! And all you can do is bicker at each other about leaving an hour late, dragging relationship comparisons and the memory of Peter into your personal measuring contests." Her voice was quiet, as she looked down at her hands, eyes filling with tears she would not shed. "It's disappointing. To think that you can't put aside your issues with each other for even just a moment, to respect whatever it is that Peter is trying to do here. I miss him. And all you are doing is muddying the waters."

After a long two minutes of silence, Emily turned back to face the wheel, clipped her belt and entered back onto the road.

As they passed the second hour, Audrey placed a hand on her mother's shoulder. "I'm sorry, Mom. Really."

"As am I," Mary added.

Jamie re-wrapped the scarf around his neck. "Me too."

"Don't apologise to me," Emily said, "apologise to each other." Mary, Audrey and Jamie looked at each other in turn.

A chorus of quiet apologies filled the cabin.

# CHAPTER SEVEN

Audrey sat in the silence of the car, her eyes focused intently on the road. It was her shift, the final shift. Hours seven to ten, the hour they had calculated they would arrive at the airfield.

She was grateful to be driving after having Jamie at the wheel for an hour. He was supposed to drive until hour eight, but Audrey volunteered out of fear for her life. Jamie was used to being driven, not driving. In the single hour that he drove, they nearly careened into a semi-trailer, crashed into the guard rails and drove into the forest of pine trees that lined the roads.

Audrey had requested a pit stop, where they had all piled out of the car at a quaint little café off the back roads of the highway. The only one around for miles and miles. They were officially in the middle of nowhere. The log building looked warm and inviting to Audrey, who leapt up the three stairs to the entrance with enthusiasm, awaiting a long anticipated coffee.

Emily followed behind her, as Mary waited at the bottom of the steps, peeling mud off of her heel.

Audrey waited at the door for her, allowing Emily and Jamie to go in first as she watched her sister battle a losing war against nature.

"Do you need any help?" Audrey asked. Her own flat boots were caked in drying mud, but she didn't mind. It was a cool, breezy day, and her striped scarf did its best to fend off the cold.

"No," Mary said, slamming her heel down on the first stair. She wore skin-tight jeans and a red blouse, covered by a white, form-fitting suit jacket that scooped at the back. Her short black hair fell straight to her shoulders, shining in the sun overhead. She was, in Audrey's opinion – and in the opinion of most others – alarmingly beautiful.

Audrey instinctively wrapped a hand around her waist, self-consciously aware of her stomach, which could have been flatter. She was so much plainer than Mary – she had mousy brown hair, which fell in light waves to the middle of her back, a face that only just passed as pretty, and could fare to lose a few pounds. "Do you want me to hold the door for you?" she asked. She looked down past her light blue jeans to her toes, as she balanced back on her heels.

"Of course not. Feminism has prevailed, you know. This isn't 1955." Mary straightened and marched up the steps. She paused and waited for Audrey to go inside, waving a hand in front of her in a hurried gesture.

Audrey had dipped her head and walked inside, shoulders stooped.

Inside, a fireplace crackled by the far wall, and eclectic tables were scattered over the floor. Old paintings hung on the walls, and the counter was deep, dark oak. A woman smiled at them from behind the bench and asked for their orders.

Audrey tried, for a moment, to pretend she was there alone. She closed her eyes and smelled the aroma of freshly ground coffee beans, and listened to the flickering of flames. The dull chatter from the patrons was a soft hum, but the sound of Jamie declaring his disgust for the place overcame any sense of peace she found there.

His voice was loud, squashing the sounds of the customers, the fire or the coffee grinder, so that there was not a single person in the café who didn't hear his complaint. Audrey stepped further into the café, abandoning her tactless brother, in the hopes of disappearing entirely. She made her way past the tables, toward a wall decorated with old photos. She scanned the faces, wondering about their stories, until her eyes fell on a large frame that held a face that was all too familiar. The face of her father.

He was younger in the photo, about thirty or so, smiling away from the camera at something that had caught his attention. Below the sizeable portrait was a plaque that read, 'Peter Wood, *who kept our doors open.*'

Audrey spun around and made her way back to Emily, asking her to follow.

When Emily saw the face of her ex-husband staring back at her, her jaw dropped open. She took a few tentative steps forward and extended a hand towards the frame. She allowed the tips of her fingers to trace the outline of the face she loved and let out a small whimper.

Jamie and Mary, curious as to their mother's disappearance, found her and simultaneously sighed. "What are you looking at all the way over here?" Mary asked. "I want to get out of this horrible place."

Emily stepped aside so that Mary could see the photo.

"What?" Jamie said. "Is that...Dad?"

Mary leaned forward for a closer inspection. "What is his photo doing here?"

A small, plump lady, walked up to the Woods, a cardboard tray of their four take-away coffees in hand. She spoke before anyone noticed her presence. "Oh, that's Peter Wood. Bless his heart."

They all turned to face her in time, their mouths open like fish.

The woman chuckled at their display and placed the coffees down on the table. "He kept our doors open, you know."

"What do you mean?" Audrey asked.

"Well, it was, let me think...oh, it must have been at least thirty years ago now. We were just about to have to shut this place down. No money, no customers. Then, along comes Peter Wood and he gives us two million dollars! Just like that! He says to call him if ever this place was in trouble."

"Why in the world would he give you two million dollars?" Mary asked.

The woman shrugged her shoulders. "He said this place was sentimental to him. Herb knows more than I do. Herb! Herb! Herbert!" Her voice grew louder with every call of his name until a ruffled old man appeared at her side.

"What's this commotion about, Beverly? I'm busy." Herb adjusted the glasses on his large nose.

"These lovely people want to know the story of Peter Wood."

"Oh," he said, brightening. "Why's that?"

"He's...he's my husband. Or was." Emily's voice was a quiver.

"Yes," Mary added, "he's our father. He died. Just...recently."

"Oh no," Beverly said, crossing herself.

"Oh my." Herb tugged on the straps of his suspenders and cleared his throat. "Well, as Bevvy's probably told you already, your dearly departed gave us two million dollars."

"Yes, but why?" Jamie pressed.

"Because, he came here after he left home, to go to college in Toronto. He pulled in on this horribly rainy day. His car was breaking down and he was feeling all kinds of lost. We took him in, gave him some food, a slice of pie and a giant cup of coffee - on the house. He looked at me real close and he said, 'Herb, when I make it, when I'm rich, I'm going to pay you back for this. I'm gonna see to it you're taken care of just like you've taken care of me.' And he repaid his debts, he did."

Even at that moment, sitting in the last hour of her shift, Audrey could hardly believe what her father had done for the small team at the little café in the very middle of nowhere. Somehow she felt closer to him, stumbling as she did upon a place that he had been to before.

As the rest of her family slept, she took refuge in the silence, wondering if perhaps she had more in common with her father than she thought.

# CHAPTER EIGHT

The airfield was small. Very small. The plane they were to board was bigger than any of the buildings. Audrey pulled into the long-term parking section, which was just a roped off bit of tarmac, and as she pulled up the handbrake she announced their arrival to the sleeping members of her family. "We're here." Her voice was weary, but enough to startle Mary, who had been sleeping with her mouth wide open and her head lolled back into the corner, against the window.

"What? Where are we?" she muttered, dizzy with the rapid lurch of her head.

"We're at the airfield," Audrey said, yawning.

Emily, curled up in the front seat, straightened and stretched her arms, as Mary quickly straightened her hair and pawed at her smudged lipstick.

Jamie was the first to get out of the car. He was halfway to the entrance of the airport before the others had even grabbed their bags from the trunk.

At the reception desk, an elderly Asian lady smiled at them beyond the large glasses that seemed to swallow most of her face. "How may I help you this evening?" she asked, a heavy accent in her words.

As Emily sorted out the tickets, Audrey took a seat in one of the few chairs situated around the room. She rested her head back against the wall, only to be told a second later to rise again as it was time to board.

The plane was of little interest to Audrey, who blindly made her way to her seat, and clipped herself in. She was more than tired, and her night of sleeping amongst her shoes was beginning to take its toll. Mary and Emily, who had spent the last three hours asleep, looked considerably sprightlier. Jamie, as usual, looked sad. His face was a constant mask of what looked like melancholy and deep concentration.

Audrey often wanted to know what was rattling around in his brain, and if it was anything of more consequence than how to improve his indie look, while maintaining a significantly less indie bank account.

The Wood family had their choice of seating, being they were the only people on the plane. Mary chose to sit at a window seat, across from Jamie. Emily sat at the very front, her legs kicked up onto the seat beside her. Audrey chose to sit as far away from her siblings as possible, to avoid any confrontations that she was devoid of the energy to join.

She peered out the window onto the tarmac, the lights of the airport blinking against the beginning of the night. She shivered with the air-conditioning that fanned down upon her and used her scarf as a shawl to warm her arms. Leaning her head against the seat, she closed her eyes.

Audrey woke with a start as Mary shouted, "What the hell do you think you're doing?"

She was standing in the middle of the aisle, her hands gripping the seats beside her to keep her steady.

"What's going on?" Audrey asked.

Mary looked at her with fury in her eyes. Her voice was a screech. "They're crashing the plane into the water!"

# CAPTER NINE

Audrey spent the next four and a half minutes in unbridled fear, until the plane landed on the water, gliding perfectly in position by the pier. Her terror, it seemed, was entirely out of place. Audrey turned to Mary, whose normally pristine and somewhat cold exterior was replaced by one of fear and horror.

She had run to her seat and buckled herself tightly in place. As Audrey rose, preparing to disembark, she looked back at her sister with concern. "It's okay, Mary," she said, extending a hand. "We're safe. It's a water plane."

Mary had, when she was younger, an intense fear of flying. With her ease at getting on the plane, just a few hours previous, Audrey had assumed her fears had quelled. Seeing her there, gripping tightly to the headrest of the seat in front of her, her hair splayed across her face and small tears smudging her mascara, Audrey couldn't help but take a few steps closer to her sister. Kneeling beside her, Audrey looked around the now empty plane, before dropping a hand against her shoulder.

"It's okay, Mary." Reaching down, she unclipped Mary's seat belt. "We've landed safely. I'm going to help you up."

Locking her arms under Mary's, she slowly lifted until her sister's thin frame was upright. She stood on shaking legs, little sobs escaping as tears rolled swiftly down her cheeks.

She wrapped arm around her waist, her spare hand dragging her luggage, Audrey led Mary out of the plane and onto the pier. Emily and Jamie were already on dry land, waiting on the grass. Mary, regaining some composure now that she was off the plane, stepped away from Audrey, confident she could walk un-aided. She straightened her coal black hair until it dropped to her shoulders in one thick curtain, and adjusted her jacket.

"Thanks," she said brusquely, clearing her throat. Audrey stepped away from her sister, who was clearly uncomfortable with their closeness, and said nothing.

"What took you two so long?" Jamie asked as they reached solid ground.

"Oh," Audrey said, filling the silence that had followed, "I couldn't get my bag out of the overhead compartment."

"Right. Here, Mary," Jamie said, holding out Mary's bag. "I got yours for you."

"Thanks Jamie." Mary's voice was quiet as she took the bag from her brother.

"So," Audrey said, taking the attention from her sister, "this is it then?"

"This is Canim Lake," Emily replied.

"Have you ever been here?" Jamie asked.

"Once. A long time ago." Emily waved her hand dismissively, unwilling to discuss it further.

Audrey turned back towards the lake. The moonlight shone down upon the surface of the water, and there was a smooth breeze shaking the leaves of the trees around them until it sounded as though the trees were whispering to her, telling her secrets they had never shared. It was a perfectly clear evening, the stars unmasked and bright; she felt as though she could almost reach out and touch them.

"Hey, space cadet," Jamie called, forcing her to turn from the image before her. The rest of her family were already heading towards the log home, which sat about a hundred feet away.

Audrey, left behind, hurried after them into the night.

As they neared the house, the warm yellow glow from the lights grew larger and brighter, illuminating the footpath that lead to the front door. "Are we sure this is it?" Mary asked.

"I'm sure," Emily replied. Her shoulders were stooped and heavy, and Audrey began to wonder if there wasn't something strange about the way she was walking. Slowly, awkwardly, as if she were suffering under the weight of a hundred extra pounds. Emily led the way up the path, which was lined with what looked like tufts of bushes in the darkness. She stopped in front of the door and raised a clenched fist, tapping it three times.

It was only a brief moment before the door was swung open in front of them, and light splashed across their faces. A warm voice, coming from the figure, whose image was inconceivable until their eyes adjusted to the light, called out to them, "Come in, come in!"

She stepped out of the way, and the Woods tumbled inside out of the darkness. Enveloped by the light, Audrey could see her Aunt Norah beaming at them, her soft features stretched into a grin. Her light brown hair was wrapped up in a bun on top of her head, and her deep brown eyes shone out behind thin-framed glasses.

Audrey hadn't seen Norah since she was sixteen. Seven years seemed to have had no effect on the vivacious woman before her, who took their coats and hung them by the door with fervour. "You all look so cold. Go sit by the fire. How was your trip? Tell me everything."

"Well," Emily began, "It was long. We started at five this morning."

"Six," Mary corrected, with an unsubtle glance to Audrey.

Audrey shrunk down into her chair and curled her legs up under her. "Sorry. It's my fault that we're late," she admitted.

"Late?" Norah looked appalled. "Nonsense. Family is never late. The door is always open. It's just so good to see you lot after all these years."

Audrey, Jamie and Mary smiled back, somewhat guiltily, having spared very little thought for their Aunt Norah over the past seven years. They hadn't known her well, and rarely saw her. Peter and Norah were close when they were younger, but as Peter had grown busier, the time he spared for his family grew sparser, and four thousand kilometres had made all the difference.

Audrey barely remembered her from her childhood, only retaining foggy memories of her visiting for a Christmas or two. When she had last seen her, it was for her father's birthday, seven years ago. He had thrown an extravagant celebration, and Norah had made the trip. The most she remembered about Norah was that she wore a stunning blue dress, which, in turn, made Audrey feel frumpy and odd.

Even now, Norah was the picture of elegance. She reminded Audrey, in both appearance and nature, of Julie Andrews. Even though it was late at night, she wore pale suit pants and a black button down blouse. She seemed to fit right in with her surroundings. The living room was inviting, with comfortable couches perched in just the right places, to accentuate the artwork on the walls better. It was pristine and modern, but somehow comforting, like an old blanket or a baggy sweater. The house, from a distance, hadn't seemed so big, but once inside Audrey noticed it was quite large. The living room branched off to the wide kitchen, complete with hanging pots, and a set of stairs sat behind the kitchen, reaching up to the second floor.

"Would anyone like a cup of tea?" Norah asked.

They each shook their heads wearily in turn.

"Oh, of course, you must all be so tired. Come, I'll show you to your rooms. Finally, someone to stay with me in this big old house."

It turned out that the log home was big enough that they each received their own room. Once inside her room, Audrey flicked on the light, closed the door and leaned back against it, closing her eyes. Exhaustion caused her knees to shake and rattled her body. Slowly, she clawed open her eyes and made her way to the bed, without scanning the room. Pulling back the covers, she fell and was asleep before her head hit the pillow.

# CHAPTER TEN

Audrey's eyes fluttered open and fell shut again. She was encased in warmth, laying on a conglomeration of clouds. Her head was resting in a marshmallow. Awakening made the least amount of sense when she felt she was curled up in the arms of Captain America.

She made a compromise with herself that she would allow herself precisely thirty more minutes to sleep. Thirty minutes was nothing, the blink of an eye. She rolled over, satisfied with her decision, straight into a ray of bright sunshine that had crept through a sliver in the curtains. Her eyes popped open and shocked with momentary blindness, she flew upright.

As her eyes adjusted to being open once again, she surveyed the room with confusion. The bed she slept on was large, covered with a deep maroon comforter. At the foot of the bed, there was a wooden chest and on the far wall was a painting of a stone cottage and rolling acreage. A window seat sat under the culprit of her early awakening; blackout curtains that covered a wall to wall window, except for a centimetre in the middle.

It took her longer than it should have to remember that she was staying with her Aunt Norah in Canim Lake, British Columbia. She heaved the weighty covers off her body and headed for the door.

As she descended the stairs, the smell of pancakes wafted around her nose, enticing her further. In the kitchen, she discovered she was the last one up, and she blushed slightly with embarrassment.

"Good morning, sleepy head," Norah said, waving at her, spatula in hand. She stood over the bench, frying pan on the built in stove, a pancake bubbling happily. The clock on the wall at the end of the stairs declared the time to be nine thirty-seven. Mary sat, fully dressed in black jeans and an expensive woollen sweater, on a bar stool at the bench.

"Morning," Audrey replied, rubbing her eyes. "It smells great."

"Well, come on and eat something," Norah said, waving her forward with the spatula. "Your mother has already eaten four."

Emily looked up from a maple syrup covered plate, a guilty smile on her face. "I couldn't help it," she said, her mouth still half full of pancake, "they taste so good."

Mary looked towards Audrey; one pancake sat hardly touched on her plate. Her expression was difficult to read, but as Audrey neared the kitchen, it became clearer. She stood up and placed her plate on the sink.

"I'm going to go find Jamie," she said, before leaving the room.

The two sisters hadn't spent so much time together since they had lived under one roof. She had been twelve when Mary had left, without concern. Clearly twenty-four hours together was Mary's limit.

Audrey forced a smile at Norah and Emily, taking Mary's seat at the bench. Norah gave her a knowing look, somewhere in the neighbourhood of pity and consternation. Her brows furrowed together before she caught herself and let a relaxed smile play across her features as she dropped two pancakes on a plate and passed it to her.

The maple syrup jug sat in front of her, masquerading as a ceramic duck. She poured a considerable amount over her pancakes and stuck her fork into the first one.

"Uh, uh, uh," Norah said, tutting. She scooped half a cup of fresh blueberries onto her plate, followed by a dollop of ice cream. "That's how we do pancakes out here." She winked and turned back to the kitchen.

"So," Emily began as Audrey started her breakfast, "what's the plan for today, Norah?"

"Well," she said, "I was thinking maybe the kids would like to see how this place runs."

Audrey smiled at the words, the kids, as if they were all waiting to be legal.

"That," Emily said, holding her fork up in the air, "is an excellent idea!"

"Absolutely not." Mary stood in front of the stable, a pitchfork in hand. Ignoring requests to change from stilettos to boots, Mary looked entirely unprepared to shovel horse manure.

"Come on," Norah said, ushering her forwards until she stood in front of a stall. "It's easy."

"No. No! It's disgusting." Mary tried to hand the pitch fork over, but Emily stepped forward and shoved it purposefully back.

"Mary," Emily said quietly, leaning close, "you will not be rude to our host. Get in there. Now."

Audrey had already plucked another pitchfork from where it hung on the wall, and was shovelling in the opposite stall.

"Come on Mary, it's kind of fun."

Mary turned to face Audrey, her lips pursing slightly. Her grip tightened around the pitchfork and she stepped into the stall, determinedly.

It was, without a doubt, the most disgusting thing Mary had ever had to do. She was a lawyer. A successful one at that. She paid people to do things like this so that she never had to. How could it be that she found herself in a position where she had no other choice than to shovel horse poo?

The smell itself was overwhelming. Mary raised a hand to her nose and took a deep whiff of Chanel Number 5 in preparation for what she was about to do.

Digging into the hay and manure mixture, Mary yanked back on the pitch fork and flung a lump over her shoulder. She sighed. It was utterly abhorrent. She turned when Audrey shrieked, dung splattered all over her back. She watched as her sister backed out of the stall and turned, red-faced, to Mary, who raised a hand to her mouth to cover her laughter.

Norah and Emily stood, mouths open, taking in the spectacle. Audrey sucked in heavy breaths. "Why did you do that?" she hissed.

"I'm sorry," Mary stuttered through hysterical laughter. "It was an accident."

"An accident?" Audrey bellowed. "Yeah. Right!"

She lunged forward at her sister, who turned on her thin heel. As she twisted, her heel slipped in a smudge of manure, and she tumbled backwards. Flailing, she grabbed onto her sister's arm for support but only managed to drag her down with her. The two landed solidly on the floor, as hay puffed up into the air with their sudden descent.

Stunned, the two sat in silence until Mary let out an ear-splitting screech. She got up onto her knees and twisted to see her backside was entirely covered in horse excrement. Audrey threw back her head and laughed, joined swiftly by Emily and Norah, who bent over in hysterics.

Not only had she had to enter the stall to clear out horse crap, but now she also had it all over her four hundred dollar jeans.

"It's on my ass!" she shrieked. "Get it off!"

Audrey laughed harder, grabbing at the sides of her stomach. Her face was contorted in a way that made the corner of Mary's mouth tilt upward. The fury in her face slowly settled until she began to chuckle, which then gave way to breath-taking laughter. She let herself sit back and grabbed a handful of dung. She plopped it down on Audrey's head and watched it slide through her hair.

Audrey's mouthed popped open in horror, before she too took a handful and flung it at Mary's face. Covered in horse dung, peppered with hay and laughing with her sister like she had never done before, Mary felt, for the first time in years, alive.

# Chapter Eleven

Audrey sat at the end of the pier, freshly emerged from the shower. Her feet dangled over the edge, the tips of her toes tapping the surface of the water. The lake was truly magnificent. The surface was glassy and smooth, reflecting the giant trees that lined the water's edge.

She could hardly believe that she had never been here before. Why had her father never thought to bring them? He had grown up here. Why would he not want to share that with his family? Or was he just too absentminded to consider it?

Audrey could almost see her father's ghost, walking around the lake, his mind in far off places like it always was. She could see his tan business pants rolled up past the ankles, the sleeves of his blue collared shirt rolled up to announce he was officially off the clock. Momentarily, she felt robbed. She imagined summers spent here as a child, playing on a swing Peter would have built for her, boating on the lake and big family breakfasts. Their summers had instead been spent at home, where they spent all their time. Peter had never been able to take any time off work to holiday with them, and, unwilling to leave her husband for great lengths of time, Emily had rarely taken them anywhere.

The most vivid holiday memory Audrey had was a trip they had taken to visit Emily's oldest friend, Jenna, in New York. Audrey was only ten, and she had never been to the States, let alone to a city as overwhelming as New York. Peter had stayed at home, on the verge of settling a new deal. It was Christmas, and for the first time, Mary and Audrey had gotten along. Jamie, ever the follower of his sister, had fallen into line when Mary adjusted her treatment of her little sister. There were Christmas decorations everywhere and a giant tree in a square. She felt happier than she had in as long as she could remember.

It was only recently that Audrey had discovered that the purpose of the trip was a trial run separation. Jenna was a divorce lawyer, and Emily was seeking her counsel.

Audrey sighed and closed her eyes. She leaned until her back was pressed against the pier, the sun beaming down on her face. She took slow and heavy breaths to try to clear her mind.

"Enjoying yourself?"

Audrey's eyes snapped open, and she screamed as she took in the image of a man standing over her. She flung herself upright, too overzealously, and lost her balance. Careering towards the water, she braced herself for the icy cold water awaiting her. Strong hands gripped her shoulders, and she was suspended in between land and water, before being dragged upright.

"Are you alright?" the man asked, as Audrey regained her breath, stolen from fright.

"Yes," she spluttered. "Fine."

"Sorry about that."

Audrey pulled her hair out of her face and looked up at the man. His face was rugged, a five o'clock shadow masking his jaw. His eyes were a deep brown; a few laugh lines crinkled as he smiled at her. He had a slight accent that Audrey couldn't place, wide shoulders, and dark brown hair that sat above his shoulders.

"No," she said, smiling dumbly, "that's fine. I'm, um, I'm Audrey."

"Ezekiel. Or, Zeke, is fine." He shook her hand and smiled.

Audrey stared back, unspeaking, an unmoving smile perched on her lips. Zeke looked at her and tilted his head. The moment went beyond awkward when Audrey realised that not only was he waiting for her to say something, but she was also still holding his hand. She ripped her fingers out of his hand, a little too quickly, and tucked her hair behind her ear. "Nice to, uh, nice to meet you."

"You too. You must be Norah's niece."

"Oh, yes. Yeah. I am. How did you know that?" she asked, chuckling a little. She stopped herself with the realisation she was no longer fifteen and such giggly responses were ridiculous.

"Norah. I work for her," he answered, taking a seat beside her on the pier.

"Doing...?"

He raised his hands to gesture around him, "This. I take care of the animals and the grounds for her. I was a veterinary surgeon in Madrid, but I moved here when my father got sick. I wanted to be closer to him."

"Is he okay?" Audrey asked, touching a hand to her chest in concern.

"He passed away, about a year ago. I didn't want to go back to the city life in Madrid, so I stayed here. I live," he pointed at a small stone cottage covered in ivy, about thirty feet to her left, "right there."

"I'm so sorry. About your father, not your cottage, obviously. The cottage looks lovely. Very...quaint." Audrey mentally slapped herself. Just stop speaking.

He let loose an easy smile. "Thank you. And thank you."

Audrey tried to return the smile, but her dry lips got caught on her teeth. While she hoped to come across as a beautiful, together artist, she instead looked like she had escaped from a mental institution. She stopped smiling immediately and looked away.

"Pretty," Zeke said.

"Sorry?" Audrey turned to face him, her cheeks flushing read. Was he talking about her?

"The lake," he clarified. "Pretty. Isn't it?"

"Yes!" she said, rather loudly. "Yes, it's beautiful. I was just thinking about what a shame it is that I've never been here before."

"Never?"

"No," she reiterated. "Never. It's a terrible loss, really."

"Didn't your father grow up here?" he asked.

"Yes, he did. But he rarely spoke about it. To me, he was always from the city. In my mind, anyway. I would have loved to have spent time here as a child. I could have let my imagination run wild. So much inspiration."

"You sound like an artist."

Audrey was taken aback. "I do? I mean, I am, but no one has ever told me I sounded like one. Words aren't really the brush I paint with, if you know what I mean."

He nodded.

"I paint...with paint." Her nose crinkled as she proved her point. "I'm, I make, I paint on canvas. Portrait, landscapes. Whatever comes to me, really."

"What kind of painter are you?"

Audrey was confused. "That kind," she chuckled awkwardly, "that paints portraits, landscapes and whatever comes to her."

He laughed. At her, she figured, certainly not with her. "No, I mean who are you? As a painter, are you emotional, like Van Gogh? Or romantic, like Monet?"

Audrey remained silent for far too long, lost somewhere else entirely. He looked like that, and he knew about art? Audrey blinked herself out of her reverie. "Oh, um, I don't know really. I suppose that's what your journey as an artist is about, isn't it? Figuring that out." She hoped she had sounded educated and mysterious, though she suspected she had failed.

"True. I'm sorry; I didn't mean to offend."

His voice was so enticing, Audrey wished he would keep speaking. Instead, he continually threw the conversation back to her. She imagined him reading a novel or an old book of sonnets.

"No, no," she waved her hand up, dismissing his comment. "You didn't. It's just, no one has ever asked me that, and truthfully, I guess I haven't given it that much thought." She paused, contemplating. "Does that make me less of an artist?"

*Excellent, showing insecurity on the first meeting. You are brilliant, Audrey. Truly.*

"Not in my opinion. I think that life is about discovering what true beauty is and creating it the way that comes naturally to you. We are, all of us, artists. In my mind, anyway." He winked at her, and her stomach flip-flopped.

"That's very poetic," she whispered dreamily.

He chuckled. "Thank you."

"So, what's your way then?"

"My way?"

"Of creating beauty. You said we all are artists, and we create beauty the way that comes naturally. What's your artistic method?"

He looked up and out to the lake. The line of his jaw was smoothing out to the length of his neck and disappearing down his white collared shirt, of which Audrey noticed the top three buttons were undone.

He was, in her opinion, entirely lovely.

"I like words, the sound that they make when they run off my tongue. *Palabras crean vida. Palabras son belleza.* They create life. They are beauty."

At that moment, Audrey quashed any romantic thoughts with the mysterious stranger. Words were beauty to him, and she had spent the last twenty minutes acting like a complete fool, babbling and stumbling. She couldn't even hope for it to have come across endearing; she was just plain awkward. As usual.

"There you are." Mary's voice came from behind her. Audrey turned to see her sister, wearing a short black dress and a cardigan, walking towards her. Her eyes shifted from Audrey to Ezekiel, and she smiled sweetly. "You've made a friend. Hello," she held out her hand as Zeke stood up to greet her. "I'm Mary."

"Zeke. It's a pleasure."

"The pleasure is mine. Audrey," she said, not taking her eyes from Zeke, "Norah and Mom want to have a word with us all. They sent me to fetch you. They knew you would have run off somewhere like a lost little puppy." She chuckled and touched a hand to Zeke's chest.

As she stood, Audrey noticed that you could see Zeke's chest through his shirt, an observation she was sure Mary had noticed.

"I should leave you to it," Zeke said as Mary withdrew her hand. "It was a pleasure to meet you." He turned to smile at Audrey. "Both of you."

Audrey waved a hand in defeat as he walked away.

"Oh," Mary called after him, "will we be seeing more of you?"

"I'm sure you will," he answered before stepping off the pier.

Mary turned to Audrey and let her eyes flutter like a character in a cartoon. "Oh my goodness. He is beautiful, isn't he?"

"Yes," Audrey answered. "He is."

"Come on," she said, walking forwards, "they're waiting for us."

As Audrey walked with Mary up the pier, she let the crushing weight of disappointment rest on her chest. To know she never had a chance was one thing, but then to know she was going to lose to her stunning and perfect sister was another thing entirely.

# Chapter Twelve

Norah and Emily, it turned out, wanted to tell everyone that they were all to make a trip into town, which was actually nothing more than a glorified trip to the General Store. They had all piled into Norah's Range Rover and listened to Norah explain everything they passed.

When they could finally stretch their legs at the general store, Jamie took off to look around without a word.

He was tired; depressed. His father had just died, and no one was even talking about it. Everyone had blindly followed the instructions, without thought or consideration, and it seemed that all they were doing was having an unwanted family holiday. He had had to cancel a shoot with Taliah Tomlinson, who he was about to make the next big Canadian model. The shoot could have been worth hundreds of thousands of dollars.

His family had barely said a word to him the entire trip; he felt like that fifteen-year-old kid he had once been, yet again. The fifteen-year-old kid with no voice, the one who just had to follow blindly, because his mind wasn't strong enough to lead him.

He looked back over his shoulder at Audrey, who stood there beside Norah like the doting puppy dog she had always been. She had, even when she was a child, found a way to get underfoot long enough that it became sweet and innocent, causing everyone to bend to her whim. He had hated her until he had finally left home, when she was fifteen. She had been closer to Peter than any of them. He always looked at her with adoring eyes, making her feel like she mattered, while all Jamie wanted was to be seen, for some recognition that he was there, that he existed.

That was why he loved to work as much as he did. There, he was recognised. He was brilliant at what he did, and people could see that. His name was in magazines, his photographs on billboards.

"Sorry," he muttered, as he crashed into someone he hadn't noticed was walking in his direction. "I didn't see you there."

He bent down to help the woman he had knocked over up off the ground. He took her small hands in his, their smooth texture like silk in his hands.

He prepared a smile for her, as soon as she straightened, but it was shot down. "Watch where you're going!" she snapped, adjusting her bag strap.

"Excuse me?" he said, a chuckle in his voice.

The woman before him had long fiery red hair, tight, springing curls framing her face. Her eyes were bright green, like watery moss - the most extraordinary colour Jamie had ever seen.

"I said," she hissed, "watch where you're going!"

"I'm sorry, I didn't understand you through your accent," he quipped. "What is that, Elvish?"

"Scottish," she accentuated slowly. "You blithering moron."

"Blithering moron? Have they never heard of manners in Scotland?"

"Yes, they have. And usually it begins with not knocking over a woman who was standing right in front of you! You made me scratch my elbow." She looked down at a gash from which blood trickled.

"Oh," Jamie said. "We can't leave that unattended. Come with me."

"What?" Her soft porcelain cheeks surrounded plump apricot lips that were pursed in displeasure. "Go with you where?"

"To fix it. You're bleeding."

"I'm not going anywhere with you." She backed away in frustration.

"I won't bite. Come on. I think you'll find me quite nice, once you get to know me." Jamie grinned mischievously.

"What makes you think I ever want to get to know you?" she asked.

"Because you find me charming. I can tell." He placed his hand on her back and ushered her forwards.

"Hardly!" she scoffed.

"Oh, just let me help you. Otherwise, it'll play on my conscience forever. You don't want to doom me to a life of regret, do you?"

"I haven't yet made up my mind," she answered. "Do you even know where we're going?"

"No, I was just sort of...setting off. You know, for dramatic effect. I was hoping you would take over once we got moving."

She laughed and Jamie noticed how her curls bounced in time with her voice. She took the lead, and Jamie fell behind so he was able to scan her in her entirety. After a few moments of his eyes wandering lower and lower, the woman came to a halt and turned.

"Hurry up, you. I don't want you lingering back there, checking out my arse."

Jamie laughed. Real laughter for once, not the fake laughter he put on to attract women or seem normal and happy. He liked the way it felt. "Sprung," he admitted, catching up with her. "Though you have nothing to be ashamed about. It's a good view."

"Did you really just say that?" she asked. "I mean, is that how you talk to women? Does that work, wherever you come from?"

Jamie laughed again. "Yes actually. Sad, isn't it?"

"Appalling."

"I'm Jamie, by the way."

"That's nice." She took off again, heading towards the store.

"Aren't you going to tell me your name?"

"That would imply I wanted you to have it."

"You don't?"

"I haven't decided yet."

"I guess I still have time to persuade you then."

"Not really," she stopped in front of the store, "because we're here."

"Right, let's go then." Jamie ascended the stairs and the woman reached up, grabbed his shirt, and pulled him back down again.

"Where are you going?"

"Into the store, to get you some first aid attention. Look at your arm. It might fall off."

"I don't need you to come with me."

"All the same, I will."

"Ugh," she moaned. "You're like a bad smell."

"What?" he chuckled.

"You linger!"

Inside, he followed her to the counter. "Hey Marty," she

smiled, "how are you today?"

"Oh great, love. How are you?"

"A little worse for wear. You haven't got a band aid or something back there do you?"

"For you, little angel, I have the whole first aid kit."

Marty dropped the first aid kit in front of her and left to re-stock shelves. She opened the box and applied an antiseptic swatch over the gash.

"Little angel?" Jamie scoffed.

"What's your problem now?" she asked.

"Well...it's just...it's a bit of a stretch, don't you think?" He winked at her and flashed a row of perfectly straight teeth.

"I'm going to do you a favour," she said, leaning close. She parted her lips invitingly. Jamie leaned closer, eyes on her tongue as she traced it along her top lip.

"Yes?" he said weakly.

"I'm going to tell you the truth."

"The truth?" he repeated.

"Yes." She pulled back and stared at him, "You look like an entitled, overprivileged kind of guy, who no one has ever said no to. So, I doubt they've ever told you the truth about your underwhelming personality."

"Underwhelming. That's a bit harsh," he said, toying with her.

"You're unpleasant. Look at your face – it's all sulky looking until you smile, and even then you're only doing it facetiously, so it's not really any relief."

"That's not very nice," he said, unfazed.

"The truth," she said, spreading a band-aid over the slice,

"rarely is." She slammed the lid of the first aid box, and turned away. "Thanks, Marty. See you later."

Marty waved his goodbyes, and the woman made her way to the door and out onto the street. Jamie stood there, momentarily stunned, before he quickly followed her.

"So, where shall we go for coffee then?"

"You are incorrigible."

"I know. So, where then?"

"I'm not going to coffee with you."

"Why not?"

"For all the reasons I just said!"

"Not liking my personality is hardly a reason not to have coffee with me."

"What is wrong with you?"

"According to my childhood psychologist, a lot."

"I'm going now," she said, turning on her heels.

"Lead the way." Jamie began to follow, but the woman turned and raised a hand. Jamie bumped into it and halted. "We're not going to coffee then?"

"Clever boy." She turned and walked quickly away.

"Aren't you going to tell me your name?" he called after her.

"You'll have to find that out on your own," she called back.

Mary walked up to Jamie and slapped a hand on his shoulder. "Another conquest?" she asked.

Jamie smiled. "Something like that."

# CHAPTER THIRTEEN

The days were long at Canim Lake, filled with a stillness Audrey hadn't before come across. She hadn't yet learned the secret of quietening her mind and letting go. While her head was filled with grief, it didn't look like she was going to learn that secret anytime soon.

Audrey had put on her boots and taken a walk the morning that she found it. Even though it was warm for the time of year, being close to winter, and being Canada, it was still quite cold. She pulled a blouse over her head and pushed her arms through a cardigan. She had set off to explore behind the house, further into the thick wall of trees that surrounded her.

She was almost to the back of the house when she saw Zeke, built arms popping out of his T-shirt, oblivious to the cool air.

"Hello," he said, spotting her.

She paused, having hoped to go past unnoticed. "Hi. How are you?"

"Great. Are you going for a walk?" he asked.

"Yeah, I was going to do some exploring."

"Let me join you." He started towards her.

"Oh," she said, holding up her hands to stop him. "You don't have to."

He smiled. "You'll get lost in these trees without me. Then what would I say to Norah?"

Audrey chuckled and lowered her hands. "Fair point."

They had been walking for twenty minutes when she noticed it; the carving in a tree. She lingered at the base of the tree and raised her hands to trace the letters. "My father," she cleared the lump in her throat. "My father wrote this." She read the words aloud. "Peter & Emily. That's my parents."

Zeke stood beside her, eyeing the names in wonder. "Wow."

"I don't know much about the only time she came here. She didn't seem to want to talk about it. But I guess she must have been young enough for tree carvings. It's funny – I can't imagine him doing this."

"How long were they together?" Zeke asked.

"Since her first year of college. They were so in love, I've heard so many stories. But it didn't last. I guess it never does. They divorced, I don't know, a thousand years ago."

"I'm sorry to hear that," Zeke said, placing his broad hand on her back. She felt warm and tingly under his touch. Electricity ran through her veins, ignited by his presence, pulsating under her skin until she felt her heart might implode under the unexpected pressure.

"It's fine," she managed to say. "Happens to fifty per cent of the world, doesn't it?"

"So they say." He dropped his hand, and disappointment caused the ends of her lips to droop ever so slightly.

"What about your parents?" she asked, trying to distract herself from the void she felt at the loss of his touch.

She knew she didn't have a chance with the mysterious man, especially when Mary was here. She knew she couldn't compete with Mary's stunning features and super model body. Compared to her she was Cousin It, the pudgy, ugly creature you keep hidden in normal society. She needed to nip these thoughts of attraction in the bud, before they became a wildfire, fuelled by her hopeless romanticism, which she could not contain.

Mary was an angel, an ethereal creature of beauty and perfection and Audrey was Plain Jane, a significantly earthier creature of cave troll proportions. Perspective. It would keep her grounded.

"My parents were together until the day my father died. They had just had their forty-third anniversary."

"Wow. Forty-three years. Were they...you know...before you?" she stuttered her way through a hope- less question.

"Yes, they were together a long time before me. I'm twenty-seven. I have four older brothers and sisters. I'm the youngest – I'm surprised they didn't name me Oops."

Audrey listened to the tone of his voice, only slightly accentuated with a Spanish accent, as she chuckled at him. "So, if you're from Madrid..."

"Why is my accent so weak?" he finished.

"Yeah," she blushed.

"My father was Canadian; my mother is Spanish. We lived between the two countries my whole life. After I had finished Veterinary School, I chose Madrid. When my father got sick, I came back here, to where they had been living for five years."

"Will your mother stay? Here, in Canada, I mean."

He paused, contemplating.

"I'm sorry," Audrey spluttered. "Too many personal questions."

"No, no," he said. "I like it. You are a good conversationalist."

She smiled weakly, mentally reminding herself – *Cave Troll. Cave. Troll. Cave Troll!*

"I think she will move back eventually. Her other two sons live there. My two sisters live in other countries. Salma lives in California, and Matilda lives in Paris."

"I've always wanted to go there."

"Where?" he asked. "Paris?"

"Yeah. It's a cliché, I know. An artist who wants to go to Paris, but there is something so enticing about it. Even before I started to paint or draw, I had pictures of the Eiffel Tower up in my room."

"You will get there," he said.

Audrey scoffed. "Yeah, I'll believe that when I land on the tarmac. Things don't work out for me the way they do for other people."

"You shouldn't be so hard on yourself." Ezekiel gripped her shoulders in both hands and stared deeply into her eyes. She shivered involuntarily, alive in his grasp. "You seem to hold everything right here." He placed a hand over her heart and her cheeks grew as hot as flames. "Let go."

They stayed like that for an age, his hand absorbing each beat of her heart, her eyes drowning in the potency of his. It was, to her, the most intimate moment she had ever experienced.

But, experiencing an intimate moment with someone you knew would never be yours was a recipe for heartache, and Audrey knew her heart was too fragile, like a tiny bird in a cage. She couldn't bear to hope and have that hope annihilated in front of her.

Audrey stepped back, blushing a deep red. "I'm not too hard on myself," she retorted, a little too defensively.

Already, the artist in her had lived through the entire relationship, including the bitter and painful end, and her emotions were running rampant, forcing her abrupt tone and shaking voice.

Ezekiel instinctively took a large step away from her, as though she were explosive or hazardous material. "I'm sorry," he said, raising his hands in between himself and Audrey. "It wasn't my place."

Audrey turned and again started walking, Zeke following a few steps behind. "I guess," she said, before a long pause, "I guess I'm sensitive about it. Sorry."

Ezekiel said nothing but stepped up to continue along beside her.

"You know," Audrey said, her mind a rapid and confusing place, "I've spent my whole life with this ridiculous idea of who I'm supposed to be and how I'm supposed to act clouding my judgement until I can't tell what's real and what's false. I'm afraid. All the time. I feel like I'm lost in this whirlwind that's tossing me around in a hundred different directions, and I can't breathe. I just want to breathe." Audrey stopped and pressed her hand against her forehead. "Oh, gosh. Listen to me. I sound insane."

"No, you don't," Ezekiel stopped her. "I understand."

Audrey heaved a deep sigh and dropped herself down on a nearby log, cracked and old, but defiantly strong. She tucked her folded legs behind her arms and rested her head on her knee. She felt the log quiver as Zeke sat down beside her. "This whole thing is insane."

"What is?" he asked.

"Us. All here for a week at Dad's old home. If this place had ever truly meant anything to him, he would have brought us here. So, why didn't he? Sticking us all here, unable to go anywhere, is the worst idea in the world! We don't get along. I've never fit into my family. My brother and sister – they've never even liked me, let alone loved me. I have no idea what he's trying to do!"

Zeke put a hand on her shoulder to calm her. Her voice had grown stringy and high, tensing with unbearable emotion. "I," she began, sniffing back the threat of heavy tears. "I miss him. And it's so stupid. I hadn't spoken to him in weeks, but now I know I can't see him, he's the only one I want to talk to. I just... I miss him so much."

"Of course you do. He was your father."

"But you didn't know him," she protested quietly. "He was a terrible father. Not always. But for a long, long time. He never had time for me. You know, I tried to call him – three weeks ago." Audrey reached up a hand to wipe away a stray tear. "I called and his receptionist answered. She told me he was busy – buried under files and that he would try and call me later. He never did. Now he's dead. Dead. As in, not living. I can't even get my head around it."

Ezekiel was silently processing the inundation of information. Audrey sighed, "I'm sorry. You don't care about all this. Listen to me, babbling. Ignore me. It's not important."

"In my experience," Zeke began, choosing to disregard her dismissal, "people rarely live up to our expectations of them. Whether those expectations are valid or not. It's then our choice what we do with it from there. Do we love them? Do we love the idea of them? The shadow? The memory? Loving someone is as much about you as it is about them. You decide in what way you love them and how much. You learn something about who you are by loving others. You learn about life; about what it means to be alive."

Audrey stared at one spot on the ground. She noticed a fallen leaf that was browning at the edges. The veins traced their spindly fingers from the base to the edges. She was entirely speechless. As she stared at the leaf, the strong and silent figure of Ezekiel beside her, she had a distinct feeling that soon she would have to decide who she was, and how she loved. She would have to make a choice. And live with the consequences.

# CHAPTER FOURTEEN

Audrey was running with all the speed her loose boots would allow. Ezekiel ran beside her; thunderous rain drops splattering down on their heads. The trees above provided little protection from the torrents that had poured, with fierce aim, from the blackening sky overhead.

Her wet hair stuck to her forehead and the back of her neck, and the raindrops all but blinded her vision. She wasn't sure what she tripped on, but she fell fast and hard, slapping down onto the dirt puddle below her. Zeke stopped and shouted her name in concern. As Audrey lifted herself slowly, he aided her. "Are you alright?" he asked.

"Fine," she said, spitting out a mud covered leaf that had made its way into her mouth during her descent. "I'm fine." Truthfully, she was far from fine. She was mortified. Her clumsiness was not something she had wished to share with Ezekiel, who continued to seem more attractive each time she looked at him. It was unfair that his beauty escalated while she continued to look increasing like her Uncle Graham. He wasn't even really her uncle. He had just been – at least once upon a time – a good friend of Peter's.

Ezekiel brushed debris off of Audrey's shoulders. As he looked down to assess the damage, his eyes grew wide, and he turned quickly to the left.

"What is it?" she asked, the heavy rain making her shiver.

"Just protecting your modesty," he answered, his eyes remaining averted.

"What do you mean?"

"U-um," he stuttered, "white."

"White?" she looked down at her blouse and gasped, horrified. Her button up shirt was thin white cotton, and thanks to her tumble, completely soaked through, turning the fabric almost entirely see- through, as it clung to her body.

Her pink bra, patterned with brightly coloured ice cream cones, drew the eye before she noticed the smooth bubble of her breast – considerable cleavage – was perfectly visible. Below that, she could see the olive colour of her skin, right down to her belly-button.

"Oh no!" she pulled her cardigan tightly around her frame, then folded her arms to hide her extraordinarily visible assets, but the damage had well and truly been done.

"I didn't see anything," Zeke lied, as she marched off in the direction of the cabin.

"Quiet," she said, holding up her hand. "That's enough embarrassment for one day, I think."

Once they had cleared the line of trees, Zeke did his best to keep up with her as she hastened towards the indoors. He could keep the silence no longer.

"It's not embarrassing," he said, a chuckle under his breath. They stopped under the cover of the porch, safe from the rain.

"Oh, it definitely is," she objected.

"Look," he said, spinning. "My shirt is wet too. You can see through it." And she could.

The light shirt was sopping, and she could perfectly see the outline of his chest. She dragged her eyes from the sight, back up to his face. "I don't need your pity," she said, an embarrassed smile playing at the corners of her mouth.

"Pity?" he looked aghast. "This isn't pity." He gestured to his highly visible torso. "This is embarrassing. We're even. Don't even look at me."

She laughed, slapping his arm, and as he joined in, she felt all the shame disappear. She felt suddenly safe, secure in his potent gaze. As their laughter faded, he kept contact with her eyes, his face telling her something she couldn't understand.

She wanted to look away and avoid the moment, which threatened to expose her as shy and afraid, but his eyes wouldn't let her. She felt the heat from his body against her cold skin. He stood close. Too close for her to retain composure. She was dangerously close to falling. Her knees quivered below her as 56she teetered on the cusp of the heady descent towards the oblivion that awaited her if she allowed herself to feel anything for Ezekiel.

Was it just her imagination, or was he leaning forwards – towards her? Maybe she was the one leaning. She had lost all sense of balance.

The door opened wide, and a shaft of bright yellow light spilled out across their faces.

"What are you two doing out in the rain?" Norah asked, gesturing for them to come inside. The moment they had shared shattered in time, splintering into pieces in front of them. Audrey looked away and stepped inside after removing her boots.

"Oh, Zeke, darling," Norah said, "would you like to join us for dinner?"

"No," he said, shaking his head. "Thank you, but I've still got a bit left to do. Bye, Audrey."

"Bye," she said, her voice hoarse and weak. She watched him disappear into the rain while it felt like a part of her fragile heart's interior was melting.

Inside, her family were perched in various places around the kitchen. Mary was inspecting the ends of her hair at the counter, Emily stirred something over the stove and Jamie was sitting on top of the bench.

"Go on and change!" Norah said, taking off her coat for her. "You are drenched through to the bone."

"Yeah, I fell."

Audrey dashed up the stairs and gathered clothes from her suitcase before heading to the bathroom. She dropped the sopping clothes into the sink so as not to mess up the floor, and waited for the water to heat.

Under the waterfall of warmth, she swam through the torrent until she had rid herself of mud and grime. As she washed her hair, her fingers caught a dead leaf. She dragged it out of the tangled strands before crushing it up furiously until it disintegrated. Of course she had nature in her hair – she had to complete the picture of a ridiculous mess. Her cave troll appearance just wouldn't be complete without forestry.

She turned off the water and wrapped herself in the giant fluffy towel. She leaned towards the mirror, wading through the steam, and wiped it clear until she could see her reflection. She stood there, unmoving, staring at herself for an age. Her long hair was sticking to her back, looking remarkably like mud.

Her eyebrows thinned out towards the end, the colour fading to the lightest brown that made her appear almost as though she only had half of her eyebrows. Her almond shaped eyes were a dark brown, just like her father's – it was a trait, perhaps the only trait, which she shared with Mary. Her lashes were long, and something about the combination of size, colour and lashes made her eyes look old. Like they belonged to someone who had seen so much more of the world than she had. Someone whose soul was weary.

She was, roughly, a hundred and fifty to a hundred and sixty pounds. In the day and age in which she currently found herself, this number was deemed unacceptable. She should be aiming for double digits and a thigh gap. These were things she knew she would never accomplish. Her fluctuating moods dictated to what degree this bothered her.

She sighed, taking in her appearance and forced a smile, which fell flat. "At least I've got a good personality," she muttered. "Most days."

"What do you mean, this one is different?" Mary asked loudly as Audrey descended the stairs, warm in her sweater. The rain had increased since she had showered, and there was the addition of quick and aggressive bolts of lightning.

"I don't know," Jamie was saying. "She just... is."

"What are we talking about?" Audrey asked, stopping at the bench and leaning against it.

Mary, who sat just a foot away, turned to Audrey and grinned. "Jamie has met someone."

"Isn't Jamie always meeting someone?" Audrey asked. The comment could have been taking abruptly, if they were talking about anyone but Jamie, who prided himself on his many conquests.

"Yes," Mary said, still smiling. "But this one is different. Apparently."

"She is! Mom!" Jamie turned to Emily, the same pleading look he always had on his face when he called upon his mother to aid him.

"Of course she's different, Jamie. I believe you. Completely." Emily raised a mug to her mouth and swallowed a gulp of hot tea.

"Thank you," Jamie said, extending his hands, as if his mother's opinion was the final say, and the others should fall into line.

"Okay, Jamie," Audrey said, "tell us about her then."

"Oh," he sighed dreamily, "where do I even begin?"

"Not with the size of her breasts," Mary said teasingly.

Jamie shot her a look, before deciding that nothing would ruin his euphoria. "She's as bright as the sun."

"Right," Audrey said, expecting more. When there was nothing but silence, she continued. "And... and what exactly does that mean?"

Jamie groaned, exasperated. "She's fiery. She's the only person I've ever met who can compete with me."

Jamie was famous for his battles of wit. He was quick with a quip, arrogant and abrasive. In his line of work, carrying his infamous name, it had become a trademark almost as much as his constant moody expression and general demeanour.

"Really? There's another person alive as satirical as you?" Mary tucked her hair behind her ear and crossed her legs. She picked up the glass of red wine, with a perfect plumb lipstick imprint of her lips on the rim, and drew a sip.

"Yeah!" Jamie was impressed, as if this was a good thing. "She didn't fall for any of my usual-"

"Tricks?" Audrey finished.

"Lines," Jamie countered.

"Oh, my mistake," Audrey said, a smile on her lips. As she looked around at her family, she realised that something felt different. She was getting along with them - all of them. She felt no desire to run and hide or to stab someone in the face with a fork. She was...happy; actually enjoying herself.

"She rejected me!" he said, a laugh in his voice and a smirk on his face.

"I thought that was a bad thing," Mary said, confused.

"No one rejects me. And she did!" He was elated.

Blank faces stared back at him, uncomprehending. Audrey wondered what that must feel like, to never be rejected.

"Don't you get it? She challenged me! She's different. I absolutely have to have her."

"Jamie, you can't have a woman. Definitely not one like her, by the sounds of it." Audrey plucked a chip out of the bowl on the counter. "You can only be with a woman."

"You know what I mean," Jamie said, waving a hand dismissively.

"What's her name, then?" Emily asked.

Jamie paused.

"What?" Mary asked. "Is it something embarrassing?"

"No, no. Nothing like that. It's just that I have no idea."

"You don't even know her name?" Mary tried to hide a smirk.

"Nope. She refused to tell me. Said that if I wanted to see her again I'd have to figure it out on my own."

"Well, what does she look like then?" Audrey asked.

"She's beautiful. Gorgeous. But not like fake gorgeous. Real. Like you could imagine her grocery shopping."

The women in the room began to chortle at his sexist comment. "That's a horrid thing to say, Jamie," Mary said.

"What? Why? That's not what I mean – I mean she's real. An actual person. Not Hollywood, or stick thin, or airbrushed. Just naturally amazing. She has the most incredible green eyes, and this red curly hair and-"

"Oh, that's Rose." Norah turned around from the oven, holding a dish of something that smelled amazing. Four shocked faces stared back at her.

"You know the mystery girl?" Mary asked.

"Yes, of course. I know most people around here. There's only one young red head with green eyes that I can recall."

"And her name," Jamie paused, gathering himself, "is Rose?"

"Yes," Norah said, "Rose McKay. She's a travel writer. Lives not far from here, actually."

Jamie stood up, too quickly, from the bench as he scuttled towards her. "Please," he said, before he tripped over his own feet, hitting the bench, then straightening.

"Are you alright?" Norah asked, slightly horrified.

"Please," he ignored her, "Aunt Norah, you have to tell me how to find her. She is... I mean she could be the one!"

Norah smiled a small, knowing smile and patted him gently on the cheek. "Well, if she could be the one, of course I'll help you."

Audrey watched Jamie smile – actually smile – for the first

time she could remember.

# CHAPTER FIFTEEN

Audrey jabbed her fork into the chicken and raised it to her mouth. She had never tasted cooking that was as good as Norah's, but even so, it was strange for her to be sitting at a table with her family, eating a meal together. She sat next to Mary at the six seater wooden table. Audrey's eyes continued to land at the very head of the table, where a single seat remained. It should be the seat in which her father sat. Aching reminders of her loss was everywhere she looked. She felt the food in her mouth turn to ash, falling out of the corners of her mouth like sand through fingers, every time she pictured him sitting there, tie loosened at the neck, jacket slung over the backrest.

She placed her fork down on the side of her plate, a sick feeling taking root in her stomach. Why was nobody talking about what had happened? It had barely been three days since he died, and Audrey couldn't remember the last time someone said his name. It was as though everyone was pretending that they weren't here under his dying instructions and that he wasn't lying in a morgue somewhere. The silence was burning a hole in her chest. She felt red heat emanating from within her, and words burst forth before she exploded, disintegrating into nothing.

"Why won't you talk about it?"

Four pairs of eyes fell on her, shocked at the volume and intensity of her words that had seemingly come out of nowhere.

"Audrey," Emily said, almost reprimanding her.

"No, Mom. I'm sorry," Audrey said, shaking her head, "but

this is ridiculous. No one is talking about Dad! He's dead! And I don't even feel like I can bring him up."

There was a stagnant silence until Mary spoke up. "She's right."

Audrey turned to Mary in surprise. Was she? Of course she was, but for Mary to agree with her was something that rarely – if ever – happened. Had Audrey just misheard her?

"Audrey is right," Mary reiterated as if reading her mind. "We're all here, in this twisted little family holiday, pretending that nothing has happened."

"Do you feel this way too, Jamie?" Emily asked weakly, staring at her plate.

"Yes, I do," Jamie said. "I honestly do."

"Didn't he say that the whole point of this was to introduce us to who he was?" Audrey carried on. "To the boy they called Peter Rabbit? I don't know about you, but I don't feel like I know Dad any better than I did when he was alive, and if I'm honest, that's not very well."

"I don't think any of us knew him very well," Mary said softly.

"I didn't," Jamie added.

Norah sat at one end of the table, her hands placed gently in her lap. Her face gave away nothing as to what she was thinking; she looked at each person as they spoke, giving them her full and undivided attention.

Emily raised her hands to cover her face and began to sob.

Audrey's stomach dropped as she watched her mother unfold before her. She sat, unmoving, with Mary and Jamie doing much the same. Her last intention had been to upset her mother, but she was dying inside, and she could hold strong no longer.

"I couldn't," Emily said quietly, her voice barely audible. She dropped her hands down into her lap to reveal her tear stained, red face. "I just couldn't!"

"Couldn't what?" Audrey asked softly.

"I couldn't face it. I can't. I don't want to talk about him because if I don't..." she paused, almost unwilling to go on, "because if I don't, it's like it's not real. It's like he's still in Toronto, working, as usual. If I think about it, if I talk about it, I'm afraid I'll fall to pieces."

Audrey extended a hand to brush her mother's hair out of her face. "I know, Mom," she whispered softly.

"I was waiting." The first words Norah spoke at the table came through crisp and clear, like a ray of sunshine through black clouds. "I was waiting because I knew how your mother felt and I wanted to be respectful."

"Waiting for what?" Mary asked.

"Waiting to talk to you about your father."

Emily rubbed her face with the sleeves of her sweater and met Norah's eyes. She nodded; a small, frail movement. Mary, Jamie and Audrey turned to Norah, eyes wide, expectant.

"He called me, about a week ago. He said he missed me." A small smile rippled across her face. "I hadn't heard him say that in years. Too many years to count. We spoke for hours. About all of you mostly. Especially you, Emily."

Audrey turned to her mother and saw a bubble of tears form in her eyes; she squeezed her hand. "He told me about the mistakes he had made, the kind of man he had become. He said that he was going to try and change. He had all these crazy plans. He told me he was re-doing his will. He gave me a set of instructions of my own. It was funny," Norah let out half a laugh as her eyes wandered, glazed with a faraway look. "I felt like something was wrong, and I think, in my heart, I knew it would be the last time I spoke to him. There seemed to be so much finality in his voice, even though he was talking about his future."

"Do you think he knew?" Jamie asked in a hollow voice.

"I don't know. Truly." Norah gave Jamie a sympathetic smile. "Does it matter?"

"Yes," Jamie snapped. "He should have spoken to us! Should have called us! If he knew, he should have done something about it – told us, visited us! Something!"

Jamie's words hung heavy in the air. He was right, and Audrey felt anger seize her. Why did he call Norah, but not return her phone call? What made Norah more important than his own daughter? She held half of his DNA, and she wasn't worth a single phone call in the last week of his life?

"Jamie, it's not like that," Norah tried to extend a hand towards his, but he ripped it away.

"What would you know?" he hissed.

"Jamie," Mary warned, holding him back.

"What did he say?" Emily asked. Her voice rang clear above the noise in their minds and fell in front of them.

"Well?" Mary said, after a long silence, in which Norah remained perfectly still, like a statue carved out of marble.

"He said he was going to change."

"You already told us that," Jamie said impatiently.

"Guys," Audrey held up a hand, common sense breaking

through her fury, "let's not attack her, okay? She's trying to help. It's not her who is to blame here, anyway."

"I don't know what you want me to say," Norah said. "He gave me instructions and said he wanted to change. He told me about you all, how wonderful he thought you were. He told me how much he still loved you, Emily, and then he hung up."

"What were your instructions?" Mary asked.

"I can't tell you."

"Excuse me?" Jamie snarled.

Mary shot him a look to silence him.

"I can't," Norah said. "Not yet, anyway. It will make sense at the right time."

"What does that mean, Aunt Norah?" Audrey asked softly. She was, deep in the pit of her stomach, furious, but there was no point in tormenting her aunt for it – she had no control over what Peter did.

"He told me not to."

"When?" Audrey pressed.

"In the letter he wrote me. I didn't want to turn this into an argument. Maybe that's another reason why I've waited. I wanted you all to be comfortable here. To have a few days of rest, where you didn't have to think about anything; where there were enough distractions to keep your mind away from it all. Maybe that was a mistake, but it's done now, and if it's my fault, then so be it. I didn't want to speak to you like this – I had it planned. So, at least let me clear the table and get you some dessert before we speak. We can move into the living room, where you'll all be more comfortable."

No one wanted to wait to hear what Norah had to say, but the woman seemed as though she were being crushed by the weight of it all. Silently, everyone took their plates to the kitchen and waited until they could adjourn to the living room, where they hoped to learn something about the boy they called Peter Rabbit.

# Chapter Sixteen

Norah was an accomplished pastry chef. She had prepared two different pies – blueberry and pumpkin. With a hot cup of milky tea and a slice of pumpkin pie, lathered in thick dollops of cream, Audrey sat on a one seater sofa, eyes forward at Norah, who sat in the middle of a three seater lounge, by Emily and Mary. Jamie was pacing by the window, his jovial mood from earlier that evening having been well and truly replaced by something far darker.

They each had a slice of pie, but they all remained untouched. Audrey suspected the addition of the dessert was just something to make Norah feel more comfortable. She took a bite to add to the façade, though she tasted nothing.

"It started with our Grandmother." Norah's voice quivered on the last word, as though the memory itself was too much for her to take. "Her name was Eva. She was the one that called him Peter Rabbit. She met Beatrix Potter, when she was younger, and she had had such an impact on her life that she became an avid collector of her books. She loved Peter Rabbit the most. She said that, in him, there were qualities that we should all strive to possess – bravery, strength, courage, love, and a little bit of mischief.

'Sometimes I can still see her, pottering around in the kitchen. She was the one who taught me to bake – I learned everything I know from her. She practically raised us. Our parents, they weren't around much. They worked and traveled so much that even now I struggle to conjure a picture from my childhood that didn't have Grandma Eva in it. That was one thing he said to me on the phone. I was sure that he was crying. I could hear him. He said that all of his life, he swore he would never be like them, that when he had kids, he would be there for them. He wouldn't work so much that he didn't know them like our parents didn't know us. He was disappointed in himself that night on the phone because he admitted that even though he had sworn it, he ended up being just like them anyway. Worse, even.

'He left for Toronto because he refused to take money from our parents. He told me that he always admired you, Audrey, for doing the same thing. Even though he never told you. Anyway, I'm digressing. The first time I can remember her calling him Peter Rabbit was when he fell from the tree house he had built with our father. It had taken four years to build because he rarely had time. But it was finally done, and Dad left for another business trip. Mom had already been gone for a few weeks. Peter was playing, and he fell out of the tree and broke his arm. He picked himself up and walked back to the house. He knocked on the front door because he was muddy and didn't want to make a mess inside, and Grandma answered. She saw this grubby little boy nursing a swollen arm, and she packed us up and took us to the hospital. Peter was so brave; I was amazed. I was pretty young at the time, but it had such an impact on me. He was in so much pain, but his courage was infectious. I cried more than he did." Norah let out a little laugh, remembering. "When we got to the hospital, she sat there with him and told him that he was her little Peter Rabbit – courageous and strong, brave in the face of adversity. She told us stories, all through the long hours at the hospital, of Peter Rabbit's adventures, ones from Beatrix Potter and ones she just made up on the spot. But, from that day, he was always her Peter Rabbit."

It was a while before anyone knew what to say. Audrey tried to fill the silence. "That's nice," she said quietly.

"He loved it, too," Norah added. "He loved being called Peter Rabbit. I was a little jealous for a long time. She never had a pet name like that for me, but we had other things to share. Cooking, mainly."

"With all due respect, we don't care about your relationship with your Grandmother."

"Mary!" Emily hissed at her daughter's comment.

"Well," Mary snipped, "it's true. I want to know about Dad. We all do."

"You're right," Norah said, apologetically, waving a hand to dismiss herself. "You're right. I got off on a tangent."

Audrey sat forward in her seat; the pumpkin pie perched on her knees. She was watching Norah intently. Her eyes were glassy as if she was about to cry, but her voice held no quiver. The lines around her face, which gave away her fifty-nine years, seemed suddenly deeper around her eyes and the corner of her pale mouth. Norah tapped her fingers on her leg, pondering her next words.

"I'm sorry," she said, standing up quickly, a piece of pie still in her hands. "I can't."

Audrey sat still, her face going pale, as her Aunt quietly left the room.

# CHAPTER SEVENTEEN

"We need to talk about the funeral."

Emily was the last person that Audrey expected to bring up the funeral, given her precarious state of denial. Perhaps the conversation the night before had somehow helped.

"That was the next part of his instructions," Mary said, dusting off her hands from croissant crumbs.

She was actually eating something. Not just poking her fork around the plate.

"What did he say?" Jamie asked.

Mary pulled out her phone and after a few minutes began reading from her emails. "*In addition to your staying at the cabin for a week, I am to be cremated. I would like a wake to be held in Canim Lake, after your week of holiday, and my ashes are, there too, to be spread.*"

"Cremated?" Audrey clarified. "Yes," Mary confirmed.

"Like, made into ash? Burned? Like a witch at the stake?"

"Jamie!" Emily snapped. "You need to mind your tongue."

"I'm sorry, Mom, but it sounds medieval! I don't want him to be set on fire."

"It's not medieval, and it's not up to you," Mary piped in. "How is it any worse than being buried underground to rot away for all eternity? This is much more dignified."

With words like rot, burned, ash and like a witch at the stake, running around her mind, Audrey began to feel a little dizzy. She swallowed hard and blinked back rising anxiety. In her opinion, what they did to dispose of their father's body was something that should have been spoken about with at least some respect.

In her mind, she tried to silence the conversation going on around her until their voices sounded muted and blurred. What was her opinion on the matter? Did she want her father's body to be buried under the earth for the worms to feast on, or did she want him thrown into a giant oven until nothing remained but dust? And did her opinion even matter? Wasn't it her father's wishes that counted? He had obviously thought about it enough to have made a decision one way or the other, and that was what mattered, wasn't it?

If he had made his decision, why were they even discussing it? Did the family that he left behind have any say over what they did to get rid of his empty shell?

When the choices were allowing his body to be eaten by ground-dwelling creatures or burnt to ashes until he was nothing, Audrey realised there was no particularly dignified way to be laid to rest. Either way you were reminded that at the end of your life, you needed to be disposed of, and there was nothing holy or beautiful about it.

Anger rose up in her chest, and her heartbeat grew like a heavy drum was beating in her ears, a battle cry to signify the march to war. How could it be that the end was so brutal? Not only did the one she love have to die, but then she had to watch him, the body he had lived his life in, be destroyed, one way or the other. It was like he didn't matter at all, as if he never even was. All that would remain of him would be memories that, as time passed, would get darker and darker. Eventually his face would be nothing to her but a black shadow moving about in the very back of her remembering.

As the days passed, echoing into years, Peter Wood would be shoved into a small, abandoned corner of her heart, brought out only on special occasions, and forgotten like old Christmas decorations. His memory would be left to gather dust, caking under years of forgetfulness.

The stinging in her eyes burned like the wildfire she could feel ravaging her chest. She felt an abrupt grip around her chest, and suddenly her breaths became ragged and shallow. Before she had had the chance to stop it, panic had risen from the depth of her stomach. She began to hyperventilate, incapable of taking in enough air, yet bringing in far too much. She clasped at the edge of the chair, her face beginning to tingle, as though her skin was electrified, rippling with shock waves that were hell-bent on her destruction.

A thousand words ran through her mind, cascading like a waterfall through her brain. She was going to pass out, to be lost in a land of darkness, smothered by the hysteria that had taken hold.

"Just breathe." Mary's face appeared over the top of her, her cool hands pressed against either side of her face. "Breathe, Audrey. Breathe."

Audrey fought for breath, an invisible force strangling her as Mary leaned closer. "Look at me, look at me. It's just like when you were younger. You're going to be okay. Just breathe. Audrey. Audrey! Calm down."

Audrey forced herself to slow her breathing. She drew in longer breaths, forced them to go deeper, to expand her diaphragm so that oxygen made its way into her bones. Slowly, the current running through her skin settled until the blackness that had formed around the corners of her eyes cleared, and she could see clearly again.

As she came back to reality, she realised she was on the ground, her back pressed against the polished wooden floors. Her head was in Emily's lap, and Mary was leaning over her, holding her face between her hands, eyes full of a compassion she hadn't seen in years.

"There you are," Mary smiled. "Hi."

"Hi," Audrey groaned. "What...?"

"You had a panic attack," Emily said, tracing her fingers through Audrey's hair.

"I haven't had one of those since I was..."

"About twelve," Mary finished. She sat back, resting on her knees.

"You used to have them all the time and then you just stopped." Emily pulled herself back up onto the couch.

Audrey felt sudden embarrassment. They were right. She hadn't had a panic attack since Mary left home. And having one now, as an adult who felt insecure enough around her family as it was, made her want to shrink and shrink until she couldn't be seen at all. Audrey had always fought with anxiety, a private battle she dared not share with another soul. She did her best to hide it, in the only way she knew how. She let her unnameable fear leak through her paintbrush.

"Mary, looks like you still have it." Emily smiled at her daughter and winked.

"Yeah," she said brusquely, before getting up and walking into the kitchen. She withdrew a glass from the cupboard and placed it under the tap, filling it.

Audrey bit her bottom lip and let out a silent sigh. She felt overwhelmingly ashamed. She shifted uncomfortably. Mary had, for reasons unbeknownst to either of them, been the only one who could ever talk Audrey down from the panic attacks that ripped through her.

The last time, when she was twelve, Mary had left home, and the attack came out of nowhere. Emily had tried to calm her, and had even called Peter for assistance, but nothing they did could stop the anxiety from debilitating their young daughter.

Finally, they called Mary, who had refused to come.

Knowing she could no longer count on her sister, who didn't like her anyway, Audrey threw herself into a hot shower and passed out under the water.

It was then she learned to pour it all out onto canvas, and she hadn't had one since then. Mary returned with the glass of water and handed it to Audrey. "Thanks," she said quietly.

"So, what set you off?" Mary asked.

"Ashes. Buried. Decisions." Audrey couldn't bring herself to say complete sentences for fear she would bring on another attack.

"Right," Mary said.

"I'm sorry, darling," Emily said, dropping a hand on her shoulder. "It's just something that needs to be discussed."

"I know," Audrey said, sipping the water. She leaned back against the lounge, still sitting on the ground. "I know. Hey, where's Jamie."

"He left," Mary said, "right around the time you hit the floor."

"Of course he did." Audrey looked at her sister, who was

staring out the window. "Thank you, Mary. Really. Thanks."

Mary drew her eyes from the window and looked down to Audrey. For the first time in years, Mary looked into her own eyes, staring back at her, and saw someone that she loved. A sister. A...friend. She didn't feel the same resentment that she had when Audrey was younger. She had hated being the only one who could help her, the only one who could calm her. They didn't get along, and they weren't close.

It made no sense that it would be Mary. It used to make her angry, furious. But staring down at her sister now, she saw someone who couldn't help it. If Mary was the only one – still the only one – who could help her, then it was her honour.

"That's what sisters are for," she said.

# CHAPTER EIGHTEEN

Audrey had to leave the room. She stood up and disappeared outside, unable to look at her family and feel the shame any longer. Her anxiety issues had, for as long as she could remember, caused people to look at her like she was insane; so fragile that she had to be wrapped in cotton.

It had become something she was expected to be ashamed of, though it was far beyond her control.

She fought her way through feelings of inadequacy as she made her way past the flower bushes that lined the footpath, and out to the garden. She didn't know where she was going, aimlessly wandering in different directions. She spotted the cottage out of the corner of her eye and, wiping a bead of anxiety induced sweat from her brow, she headed for the door.

Ezekiel opened the door, and an easy smile passed across his face. "Audrey. Hi."

"Hey," Audrey said brusquely. "How are you?"

"Fine. How are you?"

"Oh. You know."

Ezekiel looked at her curiously; aware something was wrong. "Would you like to come in?"

"Yes!" Audrey replied, too loudly. "I mean, yes. Yes, I would. Thank you."

Ezekiel stepped out of the way and let her in.

The cottage was warm, a fire flickering calmly in the fireplace on the left wall. A small rustic kitchen sat to her right and a living room made up the rest of what she could see.

"Do you want something to drink?" Zeke asked.

"No," she said, shaking her head. She crossed her arms, squeezing herself. "I'm fine. Not thirsty."

She started to pace, back and forth, in front of the fireplace. "Nice place," she said, not looking up from the old wooden floors.

There was a small chuckle in his voice when he thanked her.

As Audrey continued to pace, he leaned against the kitchen bench, arms wrapped over his chest, legs crossed at the ankles, and waited. He kept his eyes on her, the peculiar and extraordinary creature before him.

It was a while before she spoke. When she did, her words were rapid, run together until they were barely distinguishable.

"It's not fair. Why does it always have to be about the perfect people? The people who have it together? I don't have it together. I don't. I try, but no matter how hard I try, I always end up this ridiculous mess, looking like a half-drowned puppy. But, I mean...so?" Audrey flung her hands in the air in exasperation. "Why isn't that okay? Why can't I be a mess? Be a mess and have that be okay? Why do I always feel this pressure to live up to their expectations? To be this perfect version of whoever they want me to be, when I can't! I can't! You know?" Audrey stopped still where she stood, her eyes boring into Ezekiel's. He waited for her to continue, knowing she didn't need an answer.

"I hate them sometimes. I hate them for making me feel so crazy for being crazy. I hate myself more. I hate that I can't be normal, that my brain has to be a place full of evil clowns and circus creatures. I don't try, you know? I don't try and be crazy, and sometimes it feels like the only way I can get it all out is to paint it out. But I don't have any paint, I don't have a canvas, and I somehow think that finger painting in the mud won't be as satisfying now as it was when I was a kid. I mean, do you think I'm crazy?"

Audrey realised that the question was stupid. Of course he did. She was speaking too quickly, throwing her words out into the stratosphere, as though she were having a mental break. Maybe she was.

"No." His answer came crisp and clear, and Audrey looked for the signs of a lie but found none. If he didn't think she was crazy now, he would by the time she was finished. She swallowed hard before another flurry of words poured out of her mouth.

"I just keep thinking that if I try harder, harder, harder, then it'll go away. I won't have this burden anymore. I won't have panic attacks and thoughts I can't control. I won't be someone that no one wants to be around; I won't be a person who is so unreachable because she has buried herself so deeply beneath an impenetrable, bulletproof surface. I don't want to be alone, and yet I am, I feel so alone. This world is so accepting now. You can be anything you want to be, you can marry a dog, and hey, that's okay. But if you have anxiety, if you have this thing that you can't control, can't tame, you're a freak. You're a disastrous basket case. You should have seen the way they looked at me. It was just like I was a kid again. I wanted to disappear."

Audrey dropped down where she was, sitting in the middle of the floor, vulnerable and childish. She brought her knees up to her chest and looked up at Ezekiel, as if for an answer.

He tilted his head to the side, and picked himself up from the bench. He sat down opposite her, close enough that she could feel the heat from his skin and smell his cologne. She wanted to cry, but she couldn't. "Sometimes when I'm alone," she whispered, "I feel like there is a burning sensation deep within me so true and raw that I might just disappear like the sun or the moon or the stars at the end of the universe. I think that sometimes, I am the end of the world and I can't breathe because I'm underwater. There is nothing I can do but swim and swim and swim until I make my way to the surface of the water and breach into the unknown, diving headlong into the depths of an ocean so exposed and untamed that it hurts to live."

Her big brown eyes were glassy as she looked into his deep, dark eyes. She knew in the back of her mind that she should be humiliated for having burst into his home in such a manner. She should have been embarrassed about the outpouring of words that had flooded from her dark lips, but she wasn't. She spent so much of her life pretending around people; saying the right things, acting in a certain way. Hiding. It hadn't gotten her anywhere. It had just made her lonelier. Sitting on the floor in the middle of his living room, defenseless and sad, she knew that the appropriate thing to do was to stand up, apologise and leave. But she was too lost in the depth of his eyes. She found peace there, a silence that stilled the noise in her mind. She didn't want to look away, and she didn't feel the need.

Zeke leaned forward until his head was on her knees. "I see you."

Audrey bit her lower lip as Ezekiel kept his eyes on hers. She had never felt so safe, so secure and real. The words he spoke seemed shocking to her, a surprise she would never have expected. Did he really see her? Did he see who she was beyond the façades? Beyond the insecurity, the temporary insanity? Did he see her beyond the family issues, and, above all, beyond the overwhelming anxiety she had never fully learned how to control?

"You only reveal pieces of yourself at a time, to everyone, even yourself. But I see you. I see what you have not yet shown me. You are not crazy. You are not the end of the world, and you are not drowning. Audrey Wood, I see you. And what I see is beautiful."

Audrey choked back a silent gasp, her lips parting in disbelief.

Before she knew what was happening, Ezekiel's lips were on hers. He traced his hand along the line of her neck, before holding the back of her head gently, keeping her lips close to his. His hot breath brushed against her face as he drew back to hold her eyes in his.

A silent and ageless moment passed before them, where unmoving, they sat in the melody they had created. Ezekiel smiled that cool, easy smile, and pressed his lips once more against hers.

# CHAPTER NINETEEN

Audrey sat atop the black horse, whose name was Lola, her hands shaking with nerves.

"That's it," Ezekiel encouraged, "you're okay." He stood back from her, releasing the reins into her hands. Lightly, he mounted his horse, a caramel coloured creature, with one white leg. He chuckled at how awkwardly she sat on the horse, her features twisting to accommodate her panic every time that Lola moved. "You told me you had ridden a horse before," Ezekiel laughed.

"I have!" she protested. "But, I guess it was longer ago than I thought. I'll be fine in a minute."

Ezekiel brought his horse close to hers and leaned across the distance. "You must stop worrying. You have too much fear, and you hold it all in your chest. If you don't let it go, you will be buried alive by it. Do you trust me?"

Audrey nodded. "I trust you."

"Then believe me when I say that I've got you. You're safe." He stretched out his hand, and she reached tentatively for his. She felt like Jasmine in Aladdin, reaching for the hand of her rugged would-be prince.

Ezekiel brought his lips against her hand and withdrew. "Milady," he gestured to the woods beyond them, "the world is yours."

With a gentle kick to the side of her horse, she entered the woods, weaving in between the lanky trees that soared above her. It was quiet amongst the trees; she felt peaceful. Ezekiel followed closely behind her, and she felt, just for a moment, like everything would be all right. The noise in her head became secondary. The sound of the leaves shaking gently above her and the clomping of hooves along the ground was enough to drown out the storm within her.

Audrey leaned back, stretching her arms out wide, until her eyes could see only the roof of branches and leaves that hung loftily above her. Her unique view gave her a new appreciation for how green the greens were and how brown the browns were.

Ezekiel watched her, unbelieving. He had been waiting for someone like her, waiting to feel the way he felt. She had no idea how incredible she was. She had this twisted idea that she wasn't enough, that her beauty went unrecognised. But Ezekiel truly saw her; he felt the passion she lived her life with, saw the colours that exploded out of her when she spoke. He could see the turmoil that raged inside of her, and watched how she used it to make life more beautiful.

She tamed the wild winds of her heart and sailed towards freedom with every breath she took. As Ezekiel slowly followed behind her, he wished for a way for things to be different. But he could see the end was coming, and it wrenched at his chest. He shouldn't have encouraged a relationship, but there was something magnetic about her which drew him to her. He didn't want to stay away, as much as he didn't want it to end.

Audrey stopped where she was and turned her horse to face Ezekiel. He was so extraordinary. He smiled at her, and she felt her stomach flutter with unrestrainable butterflies. She could feel herself falling for him, deeper and deeper, and she feared there would be no way to rewind. She couldn't erase what had overtaken her so quickly.

She had fought with herself over him, believing that there was no way he would ever look at her twice. Especially not with Mary here. She couldn't get it out of her mind - why her? She wasn't beautiful or particularly smart or astonishing in conversation. There was nothing about her that would draw a man like him, so pure and full of light, towards her.

She kept expecting to wake up, for it all to end when she opened up her eyes from this delectable dream. If it was a dream, she wanted to stay asleep forever.

She had lost count of how many days she had been at Canim Lake. Was it three or four? Was her week nearly up or just beginning? How had she fallen so hard so quickly? This was dangerous, she knew. But there was no way she was turning back now.

"Why me?" she asked.

Ezekiel didn't understand the question. "What do you mean?

"Why did you pick me? I've spent my life in Mary's shadow. She's beautiful and incredible. When she and I are in the same room, it's her that people look at. Not me. I have fat thighs and a boring face. Why didn't you choose her?"

"Are you complaining?" Zeke teased.

"No," Audrey said, jokingly indignant. Her voice turned quiet and serious. "I mean it, though. I don't know why you kissed me. Me."

"Why wouldn't I?" When Audrey stared back at him, still unconvinced, Zeke realised he was going to have to tell her more. "When you and your sister are together, I don't see her. I see you. I see your heart, the truth about you. I see through the façade, beyond the pretend." Zeke stepped off his horse and helped Audrey to do the same. He held her waist between his hands and looked intently into her eyes. "Your face is breathtaking. Your body is beautiful. But to me, that is secondary. It is your heart that I care about."

Ezekiel leaned forward to kiss her, his lips nearing hers, when Audrey pulled away. "You don't know me."

She mounted her horse and waited for Ezekiel to do the same. She was right to pull away. He didn't know her. If he did, if he saw the mess and the chaos, the circus of her mind, he wouldn't care about her at all. He liked what she let him see and there was no way she could maintain that for any length of time. Insecurity had gotten the best of her – again.

She turned and headed back to the stables, without looking back.


"Are you okay, Audrey?" Emily asked as she walked into the cabin. Emily was sitting on the lounge with Mary and Norah, a cup of hot tea in her hands. "Where have you been?"

"I went horse riding," Audrey replied. "To clear my head. I'm sorry I left that way."

"It's alright darling, we understand. Come and sit down. There are some things we have to discuss."

Audrey sat down on the floor opposite her mother, leaning against the back of a chair.

"Okay," she said hesitantly.

"Now, because of your earlier...moment," Emily said, trying to put her panic attack in the nicest terms possible, "we used the time that you weren't here to discuss it. And we have come to a decision."

"What decision is that?" Audrey asked.

"We have decided that we have nothing to decide. We shouldn't have even discussed it. Your father wants to be cremated, and so he will be." Emily took a sip of the tea to buy herself some time before she had to speak again. It was impossibly hard for her to discuss what to do with Peter's body. "Mary called his law firm to discuss details, but it seems Peter had already planned for this. He planned very well, actually. You know your father – meticulous. He had left the law firm with their own set of instructions upon his death – they were to organise the cremation of his body, so that we don't have to leave Canim Lake. He has," she paused and drew a breath, unable to continue.

"They have already cremated him," Norah said, finishing what Emily could not. "It has already been taken care of, so that none of us had to. It was, if you think about it, quite considerate of him. Audrey, he is trying to make this as easy on everyone as possible. He knew it was going to be so very hard, and he just wanted to help."

Audrey nodded, unsure what to say.

"The funeral will be on Sunday," Emily said.

"What day is it now? I've lost track," Audrey replied.

"It's Wednesday," Mary said. "There's going to be a wake after the funeral, so there'll be a bunch of people here."

"Where's the funeral going to be?"

"Here," Norah answered. "We thought that this was, perhaps, the best place, seeing as how he grew up here."

"And you just made all these decisions while I was gone? Without me."

Emily looked down at her hands and Mary crossed her legs.

"You had a mental break, Audrey," Mary snapped. "What did you expect? We didn't want it to happen again."

"I know. I'm sorry," Audrey said quietly. "I understand."

"What do you think, though?" Norah asked. "We want your opinion."

Audrey tried to smile weakly. She didn't want to get angry. They were, in their own way, trying to help, by making the decisions without her. But it made her feel pathetic and inadequate, as if she was incapable of making difficult decisions. She wasn't a child. She slowed her breathing and tried to respond with an even tone.

"I think you've made good decisions. If that's the best thing for Dad, then, great." Audrey stood up and tugged at her shirt. "I'm going to go have a shower. I got a little warm out horse riding."

She walked up the stairs, trying not to cry. Her father had already been cremated. He had already been reduced to ashes. He no longer existed. His face was lost forever.

In the security of the bathroom, Audrey tore off her clothes and dove under the hot water. Crumpling into a ball in the bottom of the shower, she tied her arms around her legs and sobbed.

# CHAPTER TWENTY

Emily leaned her head back against the lounge chair and sighed. "I don't think she took that very well."

"Does it matter?" Mary asked.

"Mary, I know you're dealing with your father's death in your own way, but you might want to try not being so mean, especially to Audrey. She's the only sister you have."

"I'm not mean to her. I just don't see why it matters if she took it well or not. Dad wanted to be cremated, and that's what happened. He wanted a wake here, that's what's going to happen. The only thing we decided was what day the funeral will be."

"I don't think that's what Emily means, Mary," Norah said.

Jamie walked into the open plan kitchen and opened the fridge. "Anything to eat, Aunt Norah?"

"There are blueberry muffins on the countertop and some pies in the fridge," she replied.

"What are we talking about?" Jamie asked, plucking a muffin from a large serving platter.

"The funeral and wake will be on Sunday," Mary said. "And I called the lawyers and Dad has already been cremated."

Jamie shrugged and sarcastically replied, "I'll be sure to keep my schedule clear."

Mary turned back to Emily, gesturing to Jamie's unemotional response, obviously comparing it to Audrey's. "See? That's how it's done."

Mary stood up and joined Jamie in the kitchen before the two disappeared outside. Emily remained unmoving, deflated.

"Are you all right?" Norah asked.

"Of course," Emily looked up and forced a smile.

"It's me you're talking to, Emily. You don't need to pretend. You don't always have to be strong. When my husband left me, I thought that I would never be okay again. I drowned myself in sorrow every day for an entire year. I could barely leave the house."

"It's not the same."

"I know it's not the same as somebody dying; that's not what I'm trying to say. I'm just trying to say that I understand what it means to be hurting so bad you can barely stand it. He was my brother, Emily. We might not have been that close in the end, but I still loved him."

"Of course you did. I'm so sorry. We've all arrived here with our baggage and loss, thinking we're the only ones who feel anything about this. I'm sorry."

"It's perfectly understandable, Emily. Really." Norah paused, contemplating. "I think now is a good time."

"For what?" Emily asked.

"To reveal part of my own instructions. Your part."

"I don't understand."

"Come with me." Norah stood and headed towards the stairs.

"Where are we going?" Emily asked, following.

"The attic." Norah turned around and grinned.

She let out an infectious laugh that immediately lifted Emily's spirits. Norah was so full of life and understanding. Emily felt better just being around her.

Norah pulled down the ladder that would lead to the attic,

and began her ascent, with Emily just behind her.

The attic was big enough that they could stand up straight. It wasn't dusty and dark, like most attacks. It was clean, and the two windows on either side of the room let in ample light. A lounge chair sat to one side, with a tall lamp leaning over it. To the other side of the room was a number of neatly stacked boxes and a large wooden chest. The padlock on the front was open, hanging lopsided and unencumbering. Norah sat down in front of it, and Emily almost smirked at the sight of it. She was immaculately dressed, clean and pristine. It was peculiar to see her sitting on the wooden floor of an old attic.

"Come. Sit," she ordered.

Emily sat down beside her and stared at the chest. "What's going on, Norah?"

"I told you all that I had my own set of instructions from Peter. I also said it wasn't time to tell you what they were. Well, I have instructions for them, and I have an instruction for you. I think now is the right time to show you what Peter intended for you."

"And what exactly is that?"

"This!" Norah extended her arms towards the chest as if revealing the end of a magic trick.

"A chest?"

"Well, no, not the chest itself. Though, it did belong to Peter. It's what is in the chest that matters."

"And what is in the chest?"

Norah smiled, a glint of mischief in her eyes. "I have absolutely no idea."

Norah stood up and headed for the hatch to lower herself

back down to the second floor. "Open it," she said, stepping down onto the ladder. "Come down when you're ready."

Emily stared at the hatch for a long time after Norah had vanished. She had no idea what she was going to find inside of the chest that was sitting before her and, truthfully, she was frightened. She felt entirely unprepared for whatever she would find. She had cried herself to sleep every night since Peter's death, and she just didn't want to cry anymore. She felt so alone, so scared and cold, living in a world without him.

Looking back at the chest, she was conflicted. She wanted to know what was inside, wanted to see what was so important to him that he went out of his way to ensure that Norah would show her. But, on the other hand, she didn't want to face the onslaught of emotion that would besiege her. And what if this was the last thing she would ever receive from him. Shouldn't she hold onto it, unopened, for as long as possible, to preserve him somehow?

No. It had to be important. If Norah said now was the right time, then now had to be the right time.

She blinked back her emotions and put a hand on the top of the chest. Slowly, she opened it.

The first thing she saw was an old shirt, tattered and worn from years of decay. She lifted it out and unfolded it. On it was a picture of her and Peter, locked in a passionate kiss. Below was the inscription *Emily and Peter, Entering Wedded Bliss April 19th.*

She laughed and held the shirt close to her body. Peter had made two of the shirts - one for her to wear at her bachelorette party and one for him at his buck's night. Upon the finalisation of their divorce, Emily had burned hers in the backyard.

She placed the shirt in her lap and dug deeper. She withdrew his old, faded cap, a collection of William Blake's poems and a wad of photos.

She flicked through the photos slowly; pictures of her and Peter from their college days, photos from their wedding and all of their kids on the days they were born.

Emily stopped at a photo of her and Peter. They were looking at each other with eyes as bright as their futures, and so, so full of love. She caressed the lifeless image of his face and brought it to her lips.

As she opened her eyes, her gaze fell on a pile of letters. She recognised the handwriting immediately and knew who it was that had written them.

In college, she had majored in fashion design and literature. She had taken to writing letters to Peter, as often as the urge arose. She had no idea that he had kept every one. She leafed through the papers and read the words her heart had poured onto parchment. She had loved him so fully and so deeply and had never thought there would be a day where they wouldn't be together. But here she sat in the attic of his old family home, reading what she had written to a man she had chosen to divorce.

She knew she had made mistakes and divorcing him was the biggest. She just wanted him to see her again – to actually see her. Peter wasn't a perfect man, of this she was more aware than anyone. She had been so furious and hurt by him, and, she figured, rightly so. But sitting there amongst the letters that he had cherished, she felt her own failures, and her own part in the end of their marriage anew.

An envelope of thick card stock fell out of the collection of papers and onto her lap. Her name was inscribed, but she had never seen it before.

She withdrew the paper from the inside of the envelope and read it hungrily.

*Emily,*

*By now you should be sitting in the attic of the old log cabin, having looked through the contents of this chest. I had it sent here a few months ago, for safe keeping. I'm writing this letter now, and I'm hoping, if Norah does as I will request, you will have found it amongst the old letters you wrote for me.*

*I used to read them often, after you left. It made me feel like you still loved me, and I wasn't alone. I want you to keep them, and this chest, for me. I want you to hold onto it, and my leather jacket, as memory of me. If you are willing.*

*That way, I'll feel like I'm always with you.*

*I'm not dying right now. I know I sound morbid, and because I've planned all this you're probably thinking that somewhere in my mind I knew the end was coming. Obviously, if you're reading this, I'm dead. But I want you to know that I have absolutely no idea when the end will come for me. I just want to be prepared. So, I'm making plans. I'm going to try and be better, as of now, but I suppose you, sitting right where you are now, will be the judge of whether or not I succeeded. Old habits die very hard and very slowly.*

*I want you to know, above all things, that I love you. Truly and deeply, beyond all human measurement. I know you don't love me anymore, and that is the reason I never tried to win you back. You were so much happier without me, and I knew that if I really loved you, I had to let you have your happiness.*

*I treasure every moment we shared, every touch, every laugh and every kiss. You are and always will be everything to me. I'm starting to sound like the writer of those old poems you used to read to me. Do you remember? Oh, I loved the sound of your voice. It swept me up.*

*I know I've made a mess of everything. Cycling through wives like some old cliché of a man. But I do it because I'm looking for you in them. Of course, I know I'll never find you there – there is only one extraordinary version of you. But I keep trying. I can't help it.*

*I don't think I ever said it, but I forgive you. I do. It was so hard to hear, so hard to adjust, but you know I don't blame you, don't you? I'm not mad. She's our daughter. Ours. And I'm thankful for our kids in so many ways, especially because they let me hold onto you in some small way.*

*If this is it, if this is the last letter I write you, I want to make it a good one, but my mind is a vacant place right now and all I can think to say is I love you, Emily. I love you, I love you, I love you.*

*Doubt thou the stars are fire; Doubt that the sun doth move; Doubt truth to be a liar;*

*But never doubt I love.*

*Shakespeare always was your favourite...*

*Yours. Always and forever.*

*Peter.*

# Chapter Twenty-One

Norah sat on the chair in the very center of the living room, Mary, Audrey and Jamie seated around her.

"Mom," Mary called as Emily descended the stairs, "come and look at this."

"What is it?" she asked as she entered the living room.

"It's old pictures of Dad, when he was just a kid."

"He's so cute in this one!" Audrey said, holding up a photo she had plucked from the stack in her hands.

"He was an adorable kid. I remember seeing some of these when I last came here."

"When was that, Mom?" Jamie asked. "You said you'd been here once before, but you didn't seem to want to talk about it. Is it a bad memory?"

Emily sat down and folded her hands in her lap. "No, it's a great memory. One of the best. Your father brought me here for a week and he...he proposed to me out on the lake."

"That's so romantic." Audrey pressed her hand against her chest.

"Yes. It was."

Norah sensed the hurt in Emily's voice. "Emily, I was just telling them some more about Peter Rabbit. I realized I behaved poorly when I was unable to speak about him, and I thought I would share some more about him."

"That's very kind of you, Norah."

"Did you know that Dad was a lacrosse player? One of the best as his school apparently," Jamie said.

"And he got kicked out of his eleventh-grade maths class for being too disruptive," Mary added.

"He pretended to be the substitute teacher when his teacher was off sick. The person they got to replace him had come all this way, and she was furious. She spoke to the headmaster, and when he found out, he was on a week straight of detentions." Audrey laughed as she finished up the story and noticed that Emily smiled.

"That sounds like him," she mused.

"I don't want you all to get the wrong idea about him," Norah said, holding up her hands. "He was kind and considerate and so very sweet. He was my protector. I was devastated when he moved to Toronto. Do you know why he made you take the route that you took here? It was because that was the exact route he took, only in reverse, when he left here. He wanted you to walk in his shoes."

"If he was so amazing," Jamie said, "why did he treat us so badly? I think I speak for all of us when I say that all we ever wanted was his love and his approval. We never really felt like we had it, or if we did, it didn't last long."

"Peter was a very complicated man, Jamie. I don't have all the answers, but what he told me was that his priorities had become skewed. He told me he was going to spend the week planning things for when he died; sorting out his will and such. After that he said he was going to make a conscious effort to be there for you kids. He wanted to be the father he had failed to become. A few days later I got a letter in the mail. Not long after that, Emily called to tell me he was dead."

"Weird timing," Audrey said. "Creepy. Are we sure he didn't

know?"

"I'm sure," Emily said, the memory of the letter she had just read freshly in her mind. "He didn't know. It's just one of those things. Life can be cruel sometimes."

"What did the letter say?" Mary asked.

"What letter?" Audrey pressed.

"The letter she just told us Dad sent to her a few days after their phone call."

"Yes. The letter," Norah began. "It was a letter to say what I was to do, in the event of his death. In regards to all of you."

Jamie shifted in his seat. "Meaning?"

"He had things he wanted to share with you all. Things he wanted to happen for you."

"Like what?" he continued.

"I'm afraid I can't disclose the information quite like that. As per his instructions, it is to be all revealed in good time; namely, after the wake. Emily, I had separate instructions for you. I was to show you what you have just seen when I felt the time was right."

"What did you just see?" Mary asked.

Emily pressed her thin lips together before she took a deep breath. "It was a chest. Filled with old memories and a letter for me. A personal one."

Audrey tilted her head to the side. "A letter?"

"He has written one for each of you. What he wants to share with you will be in the form of a letter. Oh, Ezekiel, darling, come in."

Audrey turned around to see Ezekiel standing in the doorway. She hadn't noticed his entrance.

"I'm sorry, Norah, I didn't mean to interrupt. I was just wondering if I could speak to Audrey for a moment."

"Of course. Take her. We're done here anyway."

Audrey lingered for a moment, all eyes on her. She could feel Mary's gaze shifting from her to Ezekiel, over and over, presumably wondering what in the world he would want her for.

She stood and met Zeke at his side. "I'll be back later," she said, before stepping outside with him.

"Will you come to my place?" Zeke asked.

"Uh, yeah," she said, "I guess."

They walked to his cottage in veritable silence, which continued for the first few minutes after their entrance to his home.

Finally, he cleared his throat. "W-would you like a drink?"

"No," she responded. "Thank you."

She stood in the middle of his living area, rocking her weight from one foot to the other. The way she had acted the last time she had seen Ezekiel had been embarrassing, to say the least. She had panicked inside of a moment of fear. To let Ezekiel in was dangerous; her heart would be exposed to him, vulnerable and weak and entirely at his disposal.

But a problem far deeper than that was racking at her mind. Ezekiel didn't know her, nor she him.

She couldn't be real in front of him – if she was she would lose him. Not that she even had him. Wasn't it better for her to end it now, unscathed, before he did? He would discover the truth about her – the wreck that she was – and he would run away after her heart had been fully invested in him. She couldn't bear the thought.

"What's wrong?" Zeke asked, cracking through her reverie.

"Nothing. I'm fine."

"No," he said, taking a step closer to her. "With us."

"What do you mean? There is no *us*. We hardly know each other."

"So?" His deep eyes pierced hers, plummeting right down into the depths of her soul. He touched his hand against her arm, then brushed the back of his fingers along her bare skin.

"So?" Her voice quivered. "So you need to know someone, for there to be a relationship. For there to be anything there."

"What is knowing someone? Learning about their favorite foods? Their past? We have a lifetime ahead of us to figure those things out about each other. What I know about you, Audrey, is how deeply you care. Not just for people, but about everything. You are affected by every little thing you see." He leaned in close, his face an inch away from hers. He kissed her neck, before moving his lips to her ear. "I know you are passionate and brave. I know you are sensitive and honest. I know you, Audrey. Who you are at your very core. I learnt about you very quickly. I am patient, and I will learn the rest over time, *bonita*."

"I'm afraid," she whispered. "What if you change your mind? You are asking me to fall, when I haven't shown all my cards yet. What if you think I'm crazy?"

"You are not crazy, Audrey. You are unique. You see the world in a different way than anybody else, and that is nothing to be ashamed of. To me, you are perfect." Zeke let his lips hover just millimeters from hers, awaiting her imminent surrender.

Audrey's mind was silent. The noise had faded, affected by his closeness. She could smell his cologne as it danced around her face, and her heart began to race. Slowly she lifted her mouth until it connected with his.

Her bones evaporated, and she was, in an instant, swallowed by the intensity of the man whose waist she held in her small hands. As their lips moved in time to a rhythm they themselves created, Audrey let her fears dissipate and fell.

# Chapter Twenty-Two

"Audrey, darling," Norah said. "Would you get the door? I think someone just knocked."

Audrey closed her thick book and put it down on the seat of her high-backed, French style chair, as if marking her territory. She opened the door to a portly old man, who wore a blue cap and suspenders. He smiled, revealing a row of teeth, some of which were missing.

"Emily Wood?" he asked.

"No," Audrey replied, shaking her head, "that's my mom. Do you want me to get her?"

"Oh, no that's quite fine. I can leave this with you." He placed a heavy parcel in Audrey's hands and nodded his farewells with a tip of his hat.

"Hey, Mom," Audrey called to Emily, who was at the table, drawing. She approached her, looking over her shoulder. "What are you drawing? Is it new?"

"Yes," Emily muttered, obviously displeased. "It's a dress. A wedding dress. A client wants something brand new by next week. Can you believe it? A wedding dress of all things." She dropped her head against the table, pencil still in hand. "Ugh."

Emily was a successful designer, with storefronts in Toronto, New York and Paris. Success, it seemed, ran in the family, with the swift exception of Audrey.

"Here," Audrey placed the heavy parcel on the table. She wanted to take her mother's mind off the fact that her ex-husband had just died, and now she was designing someone's wedding dress. The parcel was just the thing. "This came for you."

Emily looked at the package and dropped her pencil. It clattered to the floor. The colour drained quickly from her face. She took the box with shaking hands, drawing it closer to her.

"What's wrong?" Audrey asked. "What is it?"

"It's..." she began, standing up from the table. "I..."

Emily picked at the edge of the tape until she had grip enough to tear it off the parcel. Slowly, she lifted the tabs of the box until a large maroon jar was revealed, nestled in Styrofoam support.

A sinking feeling hit Audrey's stomach as she noticed the contents of the box. "Is that...?" she asked, unable to finish.

Emily placed a hand on top of the urn and closed her eyes. "Hello, Peter."

Audrey unconsciously stepped back from the table. She raised her hands in front of her to create a barrier between herself and the ashes of her dead father.

"What the hell?" she exclaimed.

"What's going on?" Mary asked as she entered the room with Jamie. "Mom, you look terrible. What's happened?"

"Dad arrived," Audrey said. The words had come out of her mouth before she realised how they sounded. "I mean, the urn, the ashes. Just... look."

Mary and Jamie came to the table and looked inside the box. Silently, they took in the sight before Jamie spoke. "It's bigger than I thought it would be."

"Yes," Emily said. "I, uh, I designed it, actually."

"What?" Mary hissed.

"Your father asked me to do it, when we were married. Said

he wanted his ashes stored in something I had made, so that, at least in some way, we were always together. I didn't know he actually had it made."

"That's morbid," Jamie said.

"By courier? Really?" Audrey asked, horrified.

"Are you serious? The funeral home had his ashes sent here by *Postman Pat*?" Mary looked at the box, looking for stamps and markings to give away who had delivered it.

"Yeah. An old guy came to the door and just handed it to me," Audrey said.

"Jeez," Jamie muttered. "Do you think he knew what he was holding?"

"Probably not. Unless he opened it, which is illegal." Mary was staring out the door. Her words sounded hollow.

"Creepy."

Emily lifted the urn out of the box, ignoring her children. She placed it down on the table and threw the box to the ground. She looked up to Norah, seeking her help. Audrey had forgotten she was standing there. Norah walked over to the table and looked down at the urn.

"Good to see you again, Peter," she said. "Why don't we put you over here?" She looked to Emily as she spoke, for approval. "On the mantelpiece?"

Emily nodded. She felt sick. Bile rose up out of her stomach and into the back of her mouth. She watched Norah place the ashes of the man she loved above the fireplace. It was the strangest feeling, to know that the remnants of a man, a man who was so deeply important to them all, was sitting in the living room. He was just dust, a pile of ashes, his life burned and shrivelled until what fit in the urn was all that remained.

"I'm going to go upstairs and finish that, uh, that wedding," Emily cleared her throat, holding back heavy sobs. "The wedding dress."

She disappeared up the stairs, and moments later, they heard a door slam.

Mary and Jamie looked at Audrey, almost sympathetically, before they walked outside, continuing with their plans for the afternoon. Norah turned back to the kitchen and resumed mixing a bowl of something chocolaty. When Audrey remained unmoving, staring blankly at the urn on the mantelpiece, Norah put down the bowl.

"Are you okay, Audrey?" Norah asked.

"What?" The voice had brought her back to reality. "Yeah. I'm fine."

Norah remained unconvinced. "I know you don't know me that well, but if you need to talk about anything, you can talk to me. Anytime."

"Thanks," Audrey breathed. Overwhelmed, she turned from the living room, abandoning her book and the seat she had claimed as her own, and ran outside.

She tried the cottage first, but Zeke didn't answer. From there, she ran to the stables, hoping to find him there, brushing the horses or clearing the stalls.

"Zeke!" she called, searching each stall. She stopped at the last wooden frame, containing Lola, and leaned against the door. Lola came up to her and nuzzled her nose against the back of her head. Audrey turned and extended a hand, tracing the lines of her face.

"Where is he, Lola?" she asked, pressing her cheek against the horse's forehead.

Zeke walked into the stalls, carrying a fresh barrel of hay. "Where is who?"

Audrey turned to face him, her heart nearly imploding within her at the sight of him. "My Prince Charming. I'm sure I left him around here somewhere." She blew out half a laugh, her facetiousness a method of self-preservation.

"Prince Charming? I think I might be able to help with that." Zeke walked up to her, dusting off his hands, and bent down to kiss her. Her motionless lips caused him to pull back. "Is everything okay?"

"The ashes arrived today. His ashes. By courier. It's weird, isn't it? To send a dead body via post?" She laughed at the words that came out of her mouth. "I mean, is that even legal?"

"I don't know," Zeke said, tracing his hand down the length of her arm. "Are you okay?"

"Yeah." Audrey shrugged, unsure. "Yeah, I'm fine. It's just that he's here. He's sitting over the fireplace, like some kind of twisted Christmas elf, and my Mom, you should have seen here. She's a mess, and I can't help her because I... can't. I don't know what to say. I can't even imagine how she must be feeling." Audrey stopped and closed her eyes. "I promise I never usually talk this much."

Zeke laughed and bent down to kiss her once more. "I think you would. If you ever let yourself be comfortable around people."

"People. Ugh." Audrey shivered. "Scary." She let out a small laugh and turned back to Harriet, tracing a long line from between her eyes to her nose.

"I've got something for you."

Audrey looked back to Ezekiel, taking in the stubble that ran across his face; his broad chest, cloaked by a simple white t-shirt and his unfathomable eyes, so deep and dark she could almost fall right into them. He was, to her, extraordinary.

It took her a moment to regain her concentration. "For me?"

He nodded, a smile lifting the corners of his mouth.

"What is it?" "It's a surprise."

"Can I have a hint?"

Ezekiel took her hand in his and led her out of the stalls. "No."

"Not even a tiny one?" she pressed.

"Not even a tiny one." Ezekiel led her to the front door of his cabin and stopped. He wrapped his hand around the door handle and looked back to Audrey, who waited in nervous anticipation. "Are you ready?" His face was stone, serious.

"I think so," she said coyly, squeezing his hand a little tighter.

Swinging open the door, Ezekiel stepped back and allowed Audrey first entrance to the room. There, in the centre of the room, was an easel, upon which was a large canvas. Scattered on the floor around it were a selection of paints and brushes.

A hand flew to Audrey's mouth to cover her gasp. "You...did all this... for me?" she walked further into the room and touched her fingertip gingerly to the canvas as if expecting it to disappear at any moment.

Ezekiel entered the room and stood beside her. "I thought you could use it. You told me that you're struggling to cope, without being able to get it all off your chest, and so I just... I went to the store and..." Zeke looked down to his feet, suddenly self-conscious. Audrey's face was a mask of complete surprise.

She stood staring at the canvas, immobile.

"I'm sorry, is it too much?"

Audrey spun to face him, her lips parted, her brown eyes wide. She ran towards him, her footsteps thudding against the wooden floors. She flung herself into his embrace, and as he slowly wrapped his arms tightly around her, she squeezed her eyes closed in gratitude. "It's perfect," she whispered. "Thank you."

The smell of her hair danced around his face and for a long moment he was intoxicated. The combination of her warmth, her embrace and the subtle notes of her perfume made his head spin in a way he had never felt before. He pulled her closer to him; he could feel her heartbeat against him, as it pounded through her chest. He didn't want to let her go – this glorious and beautiful mess, this ravishing vision of a woman.

He wanted to tell her, he did. But he couldn't form the words, so instead, he kept his secret hidden somewhere behind his heart and buried his face into her neck.

# CHAPTER TWENTY-THREE

Ezekiel placed the bowl down in front of her; a serving of massaman curry and rice. The table was lit with half a dozen candles, accompanying the fire in the fireplace as the only light in the room.

"You can cook too?" Audrey asked.

"Not much. I just have a few party tricks up my sleeve."

"I'm impressed," Audrey said. "It smells amazing."

Ezekiel sat down beside her and took her hand in his. He pressed his lips against her skin and Audrey felt a tingle travel up her spine.

"It looks beautiful," he sighed.

It took Audrey a moment to come back to reality and realise that he was talking about the painting that she had begun that afternoon. The evening rain that had come each night since the day after they arrived had begun early, and the two had spent the afternoon whiling away the hours, Audrey painting and Ezekiel reading.

It had felt natural, as if they had done it a thousand times already. There was no pressure for conversation when there was no need to speak, but when conversations began, the words flowed freely.

Audrey had decided that she would paint Ezekiel, who lay on the lounge, a book resting on his raised knee. She was sure she had never seen another person so beautiful. The fireplace had been their only source of light, creating a dark, yet warm, glow. A shaft of light splintered along his chest and capturing the splendour of the moment was something Audrey could not resist.

"I had a good model," Audrey replied, winking. It was one of her best pieces, she knew. The detail in Ezekiel's face was superb, right down to the small lines around his eyes

She felt as though she could reach right into the painting and touch him. Though, as he sat across from her, she knew she didn't have to. He was right there, looking at her with those inebriating eyes.

She felt safer than she ever had.

Ezekiel watched her intently. Every move she made was a rhythm he wanted to learn. She was so far beyond his comprehension, so much more than he could ever have hoped for or imagined. Her eyes were so deep and pure, revealing the striking soul behind them.

He was falling in love with her. Too quickly. Too soon.

He had to tell her, he knew he did. But how could he? How could he shatter what he had made? He should have left her alone when she walked away from him that day after horse riding. He shouldn't have chased her, but he couldn't bring himself to let her go. There was something between them, something he could not deny. He had had to chase her.

Sitting across from her, his mind and heart was burdened with unbearable guilt, he swallowed hard and forced a smile. She would never understand. But he had to make her try. He had held this secret for too long. If he wanted to keep Audrey, if he wanted a future with her, he would need to be honest.

It was going to be the hardest thing he ever had to do. He knew that there was every chance that she was going to walk away. She would hate him, and that would hurt more than anything.

"Audrey," he began, his voice weak and pathetic.

She looked at him, her eyes overflowing with trust and hope. He braced himself to see it all disappear. He would be reviled. How could someone so pure and innocent ever care for someone like him?

"What is it?" she asked, reaching out a hand and placing it on his knee.

Her touch was electricity to his body. He closed his eyes and waited for his mind to clear. He cared about her too much to lie to her. "I have to tell you something."

"Okay."

She tilted her head to the side, her eyes growing wide and bright. It wasn't fair. He was going to lose her, and it wasn't right. Why should he have to suffer for this? It wasn't – it hadn't been – his fault.

Audrey saw the pain and conflict in his eyes. "Ezekiel, you can talk to me."

Ezekiel felt his eyes grow hot. He cleared his throat and suppressed the pain and fear that rose in his chest. "I want you to listen to me," he begged. "Don't judge me, before you listen to me. Do you promise?"

"I'll try, Zeke," she said earnestly, leaning forward. "I promise. Just tell me."

"Audrey," he whispered, taking a deep breath in preparation. "I killed a man."

Audrey sat motionless at the dining table. Before Ezekiel could speak again, Audrey's hand dropped from his knee, and she pushed herself back from the table.

"What?" she hissed, horrified.

"Audrey please," he pleaded. "Just sit down. I can explain."

"You can explain? How do you want to explain that? You're a murderer!"

"No!" he shouted. "I'm not! Please, Audrey, you promised you would listen."

"Yeah, when I thought you were going to tell me you have an ex-wife or something. Not this. Not this!"

"Audrey, you have to trust me. I had my reasons. He was a bad man. The worst. I can explain it, please just let me explain it."

"Trust you? Trust you? Are you insane? You know, all this time I thought that you were the one that would be horrified once you got to know the real me. I never once thought it would be the other way around."

"Please," Zeke said weakly. "Please. Audrey. Don't tell anyone."

Audrey headed for the door. She looked back at Ezekiel, who sat at the table, his head in his hands.

He looked old and tired, burdened and lonely. "I won't," she said. "Just so long as you stay away from me."

Zeke looked up at her; his face drawn and his eyes red. "Please," he begged.

"Just leave me alone." Audrey burst out of the cottage doors and slammed it shut behind her. She ran towards the house, confused and afraid. Of course, the one man she had begun to fall for had to be a killer. Life was back in its usual order, with her sitting at the bottom of the scrap heap, alone again.

Naturally.

She walked into the log cabin and up the stairs, grateful not to have seen anyone along the way. Locked in her room, she threw herself onto her bed and tried to absorb what she had just learned.

Ezekiel had killed a man. The same hands that had cradled her face had somebody's blood all over them. Her heart started to race, and she could feel herself beginning to hyperventilate. She held her breath and slowly blew it out again. There was no way she was going to bring on another attack because of that man. He had led her to believe that she was safe and secure within his arms. How far from the truth that really was.

She had kissed the lips of a liar, held the hands of a murderer.

He had told her that he had his reasons and that the man he killed had all but been deserving of it. What reasons could there possibly be to kill someone? And just because, in one person's opinion, a man was bad, it did not mean he was deserving of death.

Audrey rose from the bed and sat on the window seat that overlooked the gardens. She could see Ezekiel's cottage from where she was, cloaked in the moonlight that broke through the clouds that poured down rain. She was wet from having run through the torrents of water and she started to shiver, but that hardly seemed to matter.

Her heart ached at the sight of his cottage. She missed him already. There was a sudden fissure in her chest, bleeding and burning, from his loss.

She jumped when she saw the door to his cottage open. Ezekiel stepped out into the rain and looked up at her window. Her room was in darkness. There was no way he could see her from where he stood. Even so, she leaned back just a little, as Ezekiel sat down and looped his arms around his knees. He stared up at her window, unmoving, deep into the night.

# CHAPTER TWENTY-FOUR

The living room had been cleared to make enough space for the eclectic collection of one-seater chairs. An impressive selection of flowers were scattered in vases around the room, and the stagnant air was filled with quiet music from the 80's; ballads and romance songs mostly.

Emily stood by the door welcoming people she either didn't know or hadn't seen in years. Her simple black dress and tightly drawn back hair created a severe look, which Audrey figured was, in this sorrowful instance, entirely appropriate.

She knew that the only way Emily knew how to deal with emotional distress was to withdraw as much as was possible. When she was with her kids, she tried not to adopt this method, but around others, her self-preservation techniques kicked in without conscious thought or effort.

Audrey was sitting at the top of the stairs watching people mingle below. She didn't know anyone, as far as she could tell, and felt the desperate desire to flee. She wanted to run as far away as her legs would carry her.

"Depressing," Mary said, sitting down beside her, "isn't it?"

"So depressing. I thought that most people were old when their parents died. Don't you feel a little young to say your father is dead?"

"Yeah, but I guess no one is ever prepared for it."

"No," Audrey mused, "'spose not."

"This is so depressing," Jamie said, walking up to sit on the stair below Audrey.

"Really?" Mary said. "Audrey and I were just talking about how fun it is to see all these close family friends again."

Jamie chuckled and leant back against Audrey's knees. It was such a relaxed and familiar gesture that it took her by surprise.

"When do you suppose Mom will march up here and tell us to be respectful and come downstairs?" he asked.

"Give her five minutes," Mary sighed.

"Or right now," Audrey said as Emily began ascending the stairs, having abandoned her post by the door.

Her three children allowed sheepish looks to cross their faces, preparing to receive an earful. "

Ugh," Emily sighed. "Thank goodness. Hide me."

Mary burst out laughing, and Jamie chuckled.

"What?" Audrey snickered.

"I cannot stand all these boorish people, giving their apologies and saying how close they were to Peter. Pfft," she scoffed. "What a joke. Let me stay up here with you."

The Woods sat at the top of the stairs, overlooking the beginning of Peter's funeral.

"Doesn't feel like I thought it would," Jamie muttered, loosening his tie.

"Nope," agreed Mary.

"How did you imagine it would feel?" Emily asked.

"Blacker," he replied. "You know, more dramatic. I expected a raging thunderstorm outside and Dracula music."

"Dracula music?" The corners of Mary's mouths pulled down to convey her confusion.

"Give the storm time. It's been raining every night since we got here. Oh no," Emily sighed. "Oh no!"

"What is it?" Audrey asked.

"Graham is here. Why is he here?"

Mary continued her look of confusion. "Mom, wasn't Uncle Graham one of Dad's closest friends?"

"Yes."

"Then shouldn't he be here?"

Emily didn't say another word. She just stood up and went towards him.

Audrey watched as Graham smiled when he saw her. Emily didn't return the favour. She leaned in close, her face revealing her frustration. Graham recoiled at her words before Emily took him by the arm and led him away.

"What do you suppose that was about?" Audrey asked.

"No idea," Jamie responded.

"Please, everyone, take your seats. We're about to begin." Norah's voice had the unique ability to be heard in every corner of the house when she projected it far enough.

Jamie sighed. "Time to go."


Audrey, by some sense of mandatory familial obligation, was required to sit at the very front. Mary sat to her right, and an agitated Emily sat to her left. Audrey couldn't take her eyes away from the urn sitting on the table directly in front of her.

The music had stopped, and there was quiet, hollow chatter in the air. When Norah positioned herself beside the urn, the chatter stilled until the air grew thick and heavy around them. The pounding in Audrey's ears grew loud, and the rush of blood sounded like waves against a shore.

This was it. This was the funeral of her father. She felt afraid of saying goodbye, of letting go. Her week at Canim Lake was over, and they would be heading home in the next couple of days – back to reality, to normality.

It would be like none of it had happened.

"On behalf of Emily and her children, I would like to thank you for coming today. I know some of you have come a very long way, and we want you to know how much we appreciate it. The tragic death of Peter has taken its toll on all of us in unique ways, and we recognise your loss. Following the funeral, there will be a wake to celebrate his life in the way he would have wanted."

Following Norah's speech, the Pastor took to the stage and began the funeral. Audrey hardly heard a word that was said. She sat still, eyes unmoving from the urn. She couldn't stop wondering how his entire body - such a tall, strong man - could be reduced to nothing in so little time. The last time she saw him, he was lying on a metal bench, looking exactly the way he had when his heart was still beating. Now, he was a pile of black ash. Or at least she assumed it was black ash. Maybe he was more of a charcoal grey. Or maybe he was white. She wasn't sure.

How hot did the fire have to be to turn his bones to powder? And how did one even make fire hotter? Fire was fire. How did it become more than what it already is? His skin would have blistered and scarred before he was entirely incinerated. A flash of her father's face, burned and mutilated, crashed into her mind every few seconds. She wanted it to stop.

More than anything, she wanted it to stop.

She dug her fingernails into her arms to keep herself focused. The pain radiated through her skin, and her mind began to clear just in time to hear the final prayer. As everyone stood from their seats and began to mingle, she let out a breath she hadn't realised she had been holding. She felt dizzy as oxygen poured back into her brain.

She looked to Emily, who remained seated. Her face was stone cold, appearing entirely unfeeling, though Audrey knew she was feeling everything right down into her soul.

Mary straightened her black skirt and buttoned up her suit jacket. "Let's go, Jamie."

Jamie just followed silently.

"I guess I should," Emily cleared her throat and adopted a faux smile. "I guess I should go talk to people. The wake will be starting shortly."

Audrey watched her mother go. Graham tried to stop her on the way, but she simply brushed passed him, unspeaking.

As Graham walked away, he cleared the path enough for Audrey to see Ezekiel standing at the back. Her heart felt lighter at the sight of him, but she couldn't deal with him right now. He had lied to her. He had a past so daunting and dark, which she couldn't get swept up in.

She had to tell him to leave. This was her father's funeral; no place for an argument.

Audrey rose from her chair and squeezed past a number of guests until she found herself by Zeke's side.

"Beautiful service," he said quietly.

"Was it?" Audrey asked. "I didn't really hear anything."

Ezekiel saw the scratch marks on her arm. "Are you alright?"

He reached out a hand to touch the red, swollen area, but she pulled away.

"I'm fine," she retorted.

"You were too deep in your head, weren't you? That's why you didn't hear anything. Audrey, you can talk to me."

"I don't need to talk to you," Audrey snapped. "Stop acting like you know me! You met me a week ago!"

"I do know you," Zeke protested.

"Just leave. Thank you for coming and paying your respects. I appreciate it. But just...go."

"You don't understand, Audrey. Please, you have to let me explain."

"No, actually. No, I don't."

"Audrey, I-"

"Goodbye, Ezekiel." Audrey turned away and dashed up the stairs. She felt sick to her stomach. What she felt for Ezekiel was something real and raw and beautiful. She didn't want to walk away, didn't want to leave him standing there with that look on his face. But what other choice did she have?

He had killed a man.

That wasn't something that Audrey could overlook. She raced down the hall, desperate to lock herself away in her room.

"Mom?" Audrey stopped when she saw her mother curled up against the wall out of the corner of her eye. "Mom, what's going on? Are you okay?"

Emily was sobbing into her hands, her makeup running down her face. Audrey sat down beside her and wrapped an arm around her shoulders.

"It's okay, Mom, it's okay."

"No, it's not." Emily shook her head. "It's not okay."

"I miss him too," Audrey said quietly.

"It's not just that, Audrey. I didn't ever want to have to do this. But I have to now, I have to, or he's going to do it."

"What are you talking about?"

"Graham." Emily started to sob again, her voice choking over his name.

"What about Uncle Graham, Mom? I don't understand."

"There's something I have to tell you. I should have told you a long time ago, I know, but I just couldn't."

Audrey leaned in close. "You can tell me anything. It can't be that bad. Just tell me, and you'll see."

"It's Graham. He's... he's..."

"What is it, Mom? Come on."

"He's your father, Audrey!" Emily almost shouted. Her voice was gargled with tears, but the words were, to Audrey, entirely unmistakable.

Audrey withdrew her arm and pressed herself against the wall. "What are you talking about?"

"Graham is your real father, honey." Emily wiped her eyes and twisted to face her daughter. Her face was earnest. "I'm so sorry, honey, I'm so, so sorry."

Emily went to grab her hand, but Audrey withdrew violently. "Don't touch me!"

"Please, Audrey. Please," her mother begged.

"Who the hell was the man we just said goodbye to, then?" she hissed.

"He was your Dad, Audrey. He raised you. As best he could. But Graham, he is your biological father. This doesn't have to change anything."

"The hell it doesn't! How did this happen?"

"It was just one night, one horrible mistake of a night. Your father and I had separated. We weren't divorced, obviously, but we had been separated for a couple of weeks." Emily brushed more tears away, her voice on the edge of panic. "Mary and Jamie were with Peter for the weekend, and I ran into Graham when I went out for dinner. It just...it just happened. Audrey, please, understand..."

"I'm getting sick of people telling me to understand!" she shouted. "How could you do this to me? To Dad? Did he even know?"

"Yes. He did. He found out when you were sixteen."

"When I was sixteen?" Audrey clarified. "You mean the year he stopped treating me like his daughter? The year he stopped caring about me? Stopped talking with me like he used to? That was your fault? All this time, I thought it was something I did, and you know what, I guess it was. I wasn't his kid! No wonder he didn't love me!"

"That's not true, Audrey! Don't you ever, ever say that! Your father loved you. He said so, in his letter!"

Audrey stood up. She could barely breathe. "I have to go."

"Where?" Emily asked, reaching a hand up to her daughter. "Audrey, where are you going?"

"Away from you," Audrey said, brushing past Emily's hand, leaving her to sit there, weak and pathetic, immersed in shame.

Audrey thundered down the stairs and was quickly swallowed by the crowds that moved around her.

The noise in her head was loud, louder than it had ever been.

She dug her nails into her arm, trying to bring herself back to life, but she was drowning.

She saw Graham standing near Jamie and Mary, presumably catching up after the many, many years it had been since they had seen each other.

Without thinking, Audrey burst through the crowds and stood before him.

"Hi, Dad," she bellowed furiously. Before she knew what she was doing, Audrey's hand collided against the side of Graham's face, slapping him hard and fast.

Jamie and Mary stood, mouths open, incapable of reacting.

Audrey drew in hot and ragged breaths, her brown eyes raging. She looked back at Graham and noticed the same brown eyes staring back at her in sorrow and horror. The room had gone silent, all eyes on her. Aggressively, she turned away and ran out the door.

Without waiting, Mary shoved her glass into Jamie's hand and followed after her.

# Chapter Twenty-Five

Audrey stood in the middle of the yard, her hand over her mouth, suddenly aware of what she had just done.

"I didn't think you had it in you," Mary said as she came to stand beside her sister. "It was a beautiful slap. Perfect positioning and an excellent sound. The sound makes it, you know. It has to be that really loud crack for it to be any good."

Despite it all, Audrey chuckled. "Well, I'm glad you approve."

"Oh, I do. Me, I love slapping people right in their smug faces. Haven't done it in a while. It was good. I felt like I was living vicariously through you."

Audrey remained silent. She began a slow pace, walking towards the water.

"Not that I wasn't a fan or anything, of your epic badass moment there, but even I usually have a reason when I slap someone. So..." she waited. "Do you wanna tell me what your reason was?"

"No reason," Audrey replied. "Just felt like slapping someone and his face was just begging for it."

Mary reached for Audrey's arm and stopped her. "Hey," she said, "look at me. Come on. What's going on? You can talk to me."

"Oh, now I can talk to you? Where have you been for the rest of my life? You have never wanted anything to do with me! Ever! You've treated me like I don't matter, like I'm this irritation you can't rid yourself of, for as long as I can remember. So why? Why would I talk to you now?"

"You're right!" Mary snapped. "You're absolutely right. We haven't ever had a relationship. I know. I've pushed you away and favored Jamie. You've never appreciated me, Audrey! I'm the one who got you your career! I got you that job at the gallery by selling it to them for virtually nothing under the proviso you get to work there for as long as you want. I went to bat for you when Mom and Dad wanted you to study something instead of working on your art! I told them you should be able to follow your dreams, because I never could! And you've done nothing but hate me. And Dad always loved you the most. You didn't even have to do anything, and he was smitten by you. Well, until I started to make more money than you, and then didn't the tables turn?"

"Well, you know what, you don't have to worry about that anymore, do you?"

"Yeah, because he's dead. It's too late!"

"No, because I am not his daughter!"

"What are you talking about? Of course you're his daughter."

"No," Audrey whispered. "I'm not. Graham is my father."

"Uncle Graham? As in the man you just slapped?"

Audrey almost laughed. "Yeah."

"I guess that explain the, 'Hi, Dad' part."

"It sure does."

"Wow."

Audrey scoffed, "I guess you'll be happy about this, hey? I'm not really your sister, so you don't have to worry about that anymore."

"Wait. Hey," Mary snapped. "That's not fair. And that's not

true. No matter what, you are always going to be my sister. Whether we get along or we don't. Whether you hate me, or I hate you, or whatever – it doesn't matter. I don't care if your father is the Elephant Man. We're family. You're my sister. End of story."

Audrey felt her eyes sting with emotion. "Do you mean that?"

"Of course I do." Mary leaned forward and wrapped her arms around Audrey, pulling her in for an embrace.

Temporarily stunned by the out of character gesture, Audrey slowly raised her hands until they were tied around Mary's thin waist. She buried her head in her chest and felt at home.

"Are you going to do anything about it? Have a relationship with him?"

Audrey sighed. "No. I had a father. And he's dead. That's that."

"Two Kodak moments in one afternoon. Aren't I a lucky guy?"

Mary and Audrey let each other go to welcome Jamie.

"What's going on? What was with the major Fight Club moment back there?"

"Oh," Audrey said, "just introducing myself properly to my dad."

Jamie pursed his lips, giving his surly face a little more character. "Huh."

"Come here," Mary said, waving him forward.

"Really? We're having a 'hug it out' session?"

"Just get in here," Audrey said.

Jamie ran forward into the embrace of his sisters. "If you insist."

# Chapter Twenty-Six

None of the siblings returned to the house for the wake. It wasn't until the last car had driven away that they returned to the cabin and dropped themselves down on the kitchen bench.

Audrey plucked a muffin off one of the trays of leftover food. Norah had gone above and beyond in food preparations, and Audrey was glad to see there was food left over.

"Hey, pass me one of those," Mary insisted. "I'm starved."

"Me too," Jamie said.

Audrey shoved the plate towards them as Norah walked back in the room. "Where did you guys run off to?"

"Sorry," Audrey said quietly.

"Sorry? You should be – I would have run away with you. I hate funerals, and I hate wakes. You could have saved me." She winked and let out a grin.

Audrey smiled, relieved. She had expected to walk back into the house to hear about how she had ruined the wake and dishonored her father's memory.

"Was everything... okay?" she asked. "You know, after we left?"

"Everything was perfectly fine. People talked and told old stories about Peter as if they were the most important person in his life. They ate the food, drank the wine. All went according to plan."

"And Graham?" Audrey hesitated to ask.

"Yes," Mary chimed in. "What happened to Daddy-Dearest? Did he hide his face in shame and leave?"

"He did leave, yes." Norah placed glass dome lids over the trays of food. "How are you feeling, Audrey?"

"Oh," Audrey muttered. "You know."

"You always say that."

"What?"

Norah smiled and covered Audrey's hand with her own. "That's what you say whenever you're really not alright. You don't have to be brave all the time, darling."

Oh," Audrey shook her head. "I just don't want to be a burden."

"Your existence is never, and will never be, a burden, Audrey. You have a brother and sister right here who will attest to that fact. Not to mention a mother who would die for you."

"Where is Mom, anyway?" Jamie asked through a mouthful of baked goods.

"She's in the library," Norah said. "By the fire. I think she's feeling a little under the weather."

"Code for 'ashamed'," Mary muttered.

"Try not to be too harsh on your mother, Mary. She loves you – all of you. And she did what she thought was best."

"Best for her," Jamie snapped.

Norah sighed quietly. "It's time."

"For what?" Mary asked.

Norah looked down at her hands before she eyed Mary directly. "Time for the letters. For the will."

"You have the will?" Mary gasped. "Why didn't you tell us? Where is it?"

"I was just following instructions. Audrey, go get your mother, will you? Tell her what we're about to do."

Audrey was slow to stand up. She didn't want to speak to her mother. She wasn't sure she was ready to face her yet. She had lied to her for her entire life. Everything she knew was a lie. She had just been to the funeral of a man she had absolutely no blood relation with anymore.

What was the point in her receiving a letter? She felt she had no right to anything in the will. It was a family matter, and she didn't feel quite like family anymore.

She opened the door to the library and saw her mother sitting, hunched by the fire, on the lounge chair that directly faced the flames. Emily didn't look up at her entrance.

"Mom?" Audrey called from the doorway but received no response. She waded through the room and stopped at the edge of the lounge chair. Emily was curled up in a ball, makeup drawn down her face. "We're going to do the letters now. Aunt Norah said it was time. We're going to read the will, too, if you can believe it. She had it all this time."

Emily still refused to move. Tears dribbled down her face, encased as she was in misery.

"Mom, please," Audrey said. "It's okay. We can talk about it all later. Just come now, okay? I can't deal with this. I can't rescue you right now. I can't. I'm drowning in my own head. It's unfair to expect me to pick up all your broken pieces when I can't pick up my own. Come into the kitchen. Now."

Audrey turned from the room and walked out the doors.

Back in the kitchen, there were four envelopes sitting on the bench. There was one for Audrey, Mary, and Jamie, and the last envelope declared the contents to be *The Last Will and Testament of Peter David Wood*.

"She's coming in a bit," Audrey said, taking her seat at the bench.

"All right. I guess we can start the letters without her. She's already read hers. Mary, here is yours. Jamie, yours." Norah leaned forward and passed the envelopes to Mary and Jamie. Lastly, she passed an envelope to Audrey. "Here you go, sweetheart. I hope it helps. I have no idea what is in any of your envelopes. So, read them, and then we'll do the will."

Mary and Jamie tore open their letters and began to read. Audrey stepped away from the bench and found a spot on the floor. She sat and leaned back against the wall, the unopened envelope between her fingers. She looked out the window to the black sky. As if on cue, the rain began.

Audrey turned the envelope over and over in her hands. This piece of paper would be the last letter she ever received from her father. Inside, the thick card were the last words that he ever penned for her. She looked up and noticed Norah was gently staring at her, an encouraging smile on her face. She nodded towards her, as if telling her that it was okay, that she had the strength to open it.

Audrey lifted the back leaf of the envelope and pulled out the letter. She let her eyes scan the page and allowed her heart to absorb his final farewell.

*My beautiful Audrey,*

*There is a secret I have known for many years now. It's a secret I haven't wanted to share with you for fear of losing you. Maybe that was wrong, but anytime I would work up the nerve to tell you, you would look at me with your big brown eyes, eyes that look just like mine, and I would fall to pieces, unable to hurt you, while hurting you anyway.*

I'm not your biological father, Audrey. But I most certainly am your Dad. I learned of your mother's night with Graham when you were sixteen, and the news hit me so hard that I couldn't bear to look at you for a long time.

That was my most dreadful error. I'm so sorry that I allowed something so trivial to get in between us. I allowed it to affect our relationship because I was hurt, and that is something I will always regret. I came to my senses and realized that I couldn't blame you any more than I could blame your mother.

Don't be angry at her. You are my daughter, Audrey. I was there when you were born, I saw you take your first steps and I dropped you off on your first day of school.

I know I have failed as a father. I know I let you down. I know I didn't treat you the way you deserved, and I focused too much on my work. But I want you to know that, right now as I am, I am planning on changing it all. I'm going to surprise you and take you away next week for a trip. Just you and I. I guess it was the past for you, and all I can say is that I hope we had fun.

I love you, Audrey. So very much. I think you are truly exceptional. You are beautiful, and clever and oh, so talented. You make me smile every time I think of you. I admire you so much for the stands you have made in your life and for the woman you have become.

I have left the business to you, Audrey. All of Wood Incorporated is, upon the event of my death, to be transferred into your name. Jamie and Mary don't need the business. They have their own. It's all yours Audrey. I leave it to you as my way of saying that I'm sorry and that you are mine, you are so very mine. You are my beloved daughter, and you always have a place here.

*This is it, Audrey. This is my final goodbye. I love you so much.*
*Don't ever forget it.*

*You are my delight, my darling girl.*

*I leave it all in your hands, to do with as you will. With all the love*
*that I have in my heart,*

*Dad*


Audrey looked up from her letter, heavy tears blurring her eyes. She could barely breathe. What was he thinking, leaving the business to her?

She looked at Mary and Jamie, who appeared equally as touched by their letters, and dreaded their reactions. Emily walked in and sat at the counter, a painful expression on her face.

"Are we ready for the ready of the will?" Norah asked.

"Ready," Mary nodded.

"Go ahead," Jamie said.

Norah looked to Audrey, awaiting her response. They were all about to find out that Peter had left a business worth billions of dollars in her hands, the hands of an unsuccessful artist. She rose to her feet and took a seat beside her mother. She pressed her hand against her back, her father's words resounding in her ears.

Audrey smiled at her mother and nodded to Norah, "Ready."

Norah began to read the will, her hands shaking ever so slightly as she held the papers aloft.

"*I, Peter David Wood, do declare this to be my final Will and Testament, and hereby revoke all former wills...*"

There was rushing in her ears, fear in her bones. Audrey sat beside her mother, shaking, as Norah read off the list of what had been left to his family.

Emily would inherit his apartment in the city, including the contents, as well as a lump sum of eight million dollars. Jamie would receive Peter's first camera, an ancient old thing with extreme sentimental value, two houses he owned outside of the city and a lump sum of two million dollars.

Mary sat patiently, waiting for her turn. Audrey could hear her tapping her heels on the floor. Mary was to receive the rest of his real estate investments – two large homes, both in the city – his collection of first edition novels and a lump sum of two million dollars.

"What about Wood Inc.?" Mary asked. "What's happening with that?"

Norah continued to read, silently, until she understood. "It's Audrey's."

"What?" Mary snarled. "Give me that." Mary snatched the will out of Norah's hands and scanned the page. "It says here that he leaves Audrey Wood Incorporated. All of it. It's hers."

"Why?" Jamie asked, surprised, yet unoffended.

"Why the hell would he do that?" Mary bellowed. She could hardly see straight. Confusion scattered her thoughts.

"I don't know," Audrey said. "I don't know why he did it. Mary, calm down." Mary had shoved herself out of her seat and was heading for the door.

"Don't even speak to me," she snarled before disappearing.

# Chapter Twenty-Seven

Mary couldn't think of anything to do but run. She wanted to get away, away from all of it. She took off at a sprint, the ever present evening rain stinging her face. It was a moment before she realised that she was heading for the pier, where a rowboat was tied, bobbing in the water.

Without thinking, she threw herself into the boat, untied it, and pushed the oars through the water. Her mind was torturing her, devising ways to bring her to her knees. Everything she had worked for, everything she had wanted, had been taken away from her in one fell swoop. She had become a lawyer for him, worked as hard as she did for him. She didn't even want to be a lawyer in the beginning. She had other plans – she wanted to write novels. She wanted to travel. But she had never had the chance to do anything beyond the enclosed walls of her father's expectations. And this – this was how he repaid her? After everything she had done for him, for the woman she had become, the money she had made.

Fury caused wet tears to bubble out of her eyes as she forced her way violently through the water.

The dark night seemed to encase her, a heavy weight on her chest that refused to surrender. She battled feelings of claustrophobia as she drew her oars through the water, dragging herself further out onto the lake. The stars hung aggressively overhead, looking down on her with pity and shame. A manicured nail snapped against the hard wood, and she felt some sense of satisfaction. She dropped the oars and ripped off her Hermes scarf, throwing it into the water. Taking her Jimmy Choos in her hands, she tore them off of her feet and flung them into the air with all the power she could muster. The thunk, as they hit the water, seemed to lift some of the weight sitting on her chest. Systematically, Mary removed everything of value - earrings, necklace, bracelet and anklet and dropped them into the water.

She was shedding a second skin.

She had wasted her life, every moment of it, trying to be what she thought her father wanted her to be. Audrey, who had never strived to be what Peter expected, was the one he had loved the most, and leaving the business to her was proof of that. The hours she had spent studying law instead of actually living her life, the years she had spent building a business, the effort she placed into her perfection – none of it was worth it.

Flashing in front of her were images of a life that she could have lived. A life of freedom. She could have been writing in Europe, a free spirit carving her way through the world, with nothing but a pen, paper and a backpack.

She could have met a man overseas who would show her what life really meant. She could have had a fairy tale, kids. Love. Instead, she had a full bank account and an empty heart, a big office and a small life.

Sitting there in the darkness, stripped of her glory, she felt closer to herself than she ever had. The heavy burden that lay weight upon her shoulders had evaporated, leaving bare memories in its wake. She was, at that moment, who she wanted to be.

She wanted to run and hide and leave and disappear, all at once. The thought of returning to land made her heart ache – she couldn't go back to captivity.

"Mary!"

She heard her name shouted over the ripples. Blackened figures hovered by the water's edge, beckoning her home.

"Mary!"

The voice was Audrey's. Even from this distance, she could pick out her sister's voice. Mary couldn't; she couldn't go back to face her, not after everything that had happened, and especially not after running away. She would stay here, embraced by the water.

A flash of lightning splintered the night sky, illuminating the world around her for an instant in a grey light, bringing everything to life as ghosts, abandoned echoes.

"Come back!" This time it was Jamie. "It's not safe!"

Mary pierced the water's skin with the oars with more ferocity, going farther and farther. Jamie was right – it wasn't safe. In that instant, Mary realised she was exactly where she wanted to be.

The moment she returned to land, she would return to reality, to the person she had to be and the façade she had put up. The swollen bruise in the pit of her stomach, the empty misery that desolated her mind, would fall back upon her and this time she feared she would not survive the torture. Here she was free, so here was where she had to remain.

Mary stopped rowing and looked up to the sky, littered as it was with the scattered stars that had found a way to break through the storm clouds. Raindrops caressed her face, and she imagined for a moment that her father was there with her, seeing who she was for the very first time and approving. She opened her mouth and breathed in the cool air, tainted with the oppression of a storm, before looking back to her family on the land.

It would be better this way. She knew it would.

Mary stood to her feet, barely rocking the boat, and peered out over the water.

It was better to lose the person that they accepted, then have a different person come back to shore – someone they wouldn't recognise. She couldn't – wouldn't – face another day trapped in the skin of the tyrant, the perfect, Mary Wood.

The water was rough with the heavy breeze that accompanied the lightning. Rumbles of thunder reverberated off the trees, sounding thick and heavy in her ears. She felt so far away from peace, so far removed from happiness. But she wouldn't risk losing herself again, wouldn't go back.

Mary wiped away savage tears and stepped over the edge of the boat, disappearing below the water's surface.

Standing in the heavy rain, Audrey watched the body of her sister drop into the water, lit up by a sudden splinter of lightning. Her mother screamed a bloody shout, her voice all but drowned out by the following crack of thunder. Jamie stood motionless, breathless.

Audrey threw off her black sweater and ripped off her boots, so as not to be weighted down. She turned to the pier and sprinted along the rough wood, throwing herself off the edge with all the force she could muster. She hit the icy water, a thousand knives piercing her skin, shattering her mind into a million pieces. She fought to concentrate as the arctic water enveloped her.

Audrey drew her arms through the water, catapulting herself forward. She didn't have long to get to her, didn't have long to save her. Her body burned with the cold and from the exertion as she tried with all her might to make it through the choppy water, exacerbated by the storm.

She stopped to get her bearings. The boat was straight ahead, about fifty metres. Taking a deep breath, she dived back into a rapid stroke.

She was going to run out of time. Mary was going to die.

Audrey realised in that moment that the chances were that she was going to die as well. She pressed on harder. If she was going to die, she was going to die trying to save her sister. Her black pants, soaked through, were heavy in the water, slowing her down. She didn't have time to tear them off. She kept swimming, ever harder.

A memory broke through the cold and the wet, and the fear, filling her mind until she could no longer see the black water in front of her. It was a memory from the holiday they had had in New York over Christmas.

It wasn't an earth-shattering memory, just a memory of two sisters having breakfast at Tiffany's after watching the movie huddled in bed the night before. They had gotten dressed up in their nicest clothes, bought a bagel each, and sat on the ground outside the building. They ate, and sat there talking and laughing as if they were best friends and things were always going to be that way.

Without realising, Audrey had stopped moving. Her lungs were burning, her chest aching, and her mind no longer spurred her on. She had never been a brilliant swimmer. She had dived into the water without thought or consideration.

She stared into the emptiness of the dark water, unmoving, unbreathing. She was out of energy, out of strength. The icy water was so harsh against her body that it limited her, broke her.

This was it. She was going to die.

She was going to let Mary down. Her family was not only going to lose Peter, but they were going to lose her and Mary as well. They wouldn't recover. It would destroy them.

No.

Not today.

Audrey shifted in the water, first moving one arm slowly, before moving the other. She lifted herself and gasped for breath. She looked ahead. The boat was ten metres away. Her arms slapped the water, and her speed increased as her determination became paramount. She drug herself through the water with the kind of fervency that comes from the end of life, the desperation of a dying woman.

She was going to make it. Audrey was going to make it to be by her sister's side.

Closer and closer she came before her arm connected with the side of the boat. She heaved in burning breaths, desperate for air and looked around. The rain slapped her face and blurred her vision. Lightning raged above her, the thundering of the heavens filling her ears. The water seemed empty, devoid of the life she searched for desperately. She swam around the boat; her arms outstretched, reaching for her sister.

She was nowhere to be found. Audrey stretched the perimeter, looking left and right, front and back, to find her.

"Mary!" she shouted. "Mary!" Her voice was ruined, choked by the water and the cold. "Mary! Where are you?"

Hot tears streamed down her face, a violent contrast with the frigid wind that burned her frozen face. She had made it; she was here. She could save her, if only she could find her.

"Please," Audrey prayed. "Please, please, please, please.'"

It was then that her eyes fell on something floating in the water, just a few feet away. "Mary!" Audrey shouted in elation. "Mary, I'm coming! I'm coming!"

Audrey waded through the water, closing the gap between herself and Mary as quickly as she could.

As the lightning struck again, the light revealed a body floating, face down, in the rough lake. Audrey reached her sister and reefed her body until her face was out of the water. Eyes closed, Mary's unflinching face was battered by the rain as Audrey tried to haul her body through the water. She spat out water as choppy tufts slapped her in the face. The boat wasn't far.

"Stay with me, Mary," Audrey begged. "Stay with me. I'm right here."

Audrey grabbed the side of the boat, relief flooding her bones. She looped her arms under Mary and tried to lift her into the small, weak boat, but couldn't. She deliberated for a moment, panic starting to creep into her chest, and let her sister's body go. Audrey tried to pull herself into the boat, but it continued to flip, as weak and old as it was. She tried, over and over, but time and again she failed. Mary's body floated alongside her, and with every attempt at getting in the boat, she was pushed a little further away.

Audrey screamed, a blood-curdling wail, silenced by her croaking voice, fear and frustration mixing toxically inside of her. She reached for Mary, who was no longer within an arms distance away.

Audrey pressed her head against the side of the boat, hanging on for dear life, and then let go.

She swam across to Mary and held her up, every part of her body screaming in agony. She couldn't get in the boat, and she couldn't get Mary in the boat. She had made it, she had reached her sister, but even now she couldn't save her.

"Help," Audrey moaned. "Help me!" Her voice was weak and empty, carried away by the wind. Land seemed so far away. She couldn't see her family, but she hoped they were still standing there, still with her in some small way.

*Swim.*

The thought didn't come from her consciousness. She couldn't say where it came from, but she heard the word in her mind as clear and as crisp as if she had said it aloud.

*Swim.*

"I can't," Audrey cried, sobbing into her sister's wet hair. "I can't."

*Swim!*

Audrey shouted again, a bubble of ferocity escaping her lips in the form of an angry growl. She had to swim. It was her only chance.

Audrey wrapped an arm around Mary's chest and used her other arm to slowly bring herself forward.

Her movements were slow and heavy, but she was moving.

"I'm coming," she whispered. "I'm coming. I'm going to

make it."

Raking in air, her lungs were scorched, her muscles enfeebled. Slowly, so slowly, she drew herself and Mary through the rough water.

"Don't you die," Audrey gasped. "Don't you die, Mary or so help me, I'm going to kill you."

Audrey's vision began to blur. Her heart was throbbing inside her chest in a way that told her that any minute it was going to give out. She could see land, almost make out the shapes of her family, but she could go no further. She stopped moving, her arms no longer taking her through the water. The waves moved her until she was flat on her back, staring up at the dark, clouded sky. She rested Mary against her torso, her eyes still closed and unseeing.

"I'm sorry," she said into the air. "I'm sorry. I couldn't. I'm sorry."

She watched the forks of lightning pour through the sky and couldn't help but think about how truly beautiful it was. Bolts of pure electricity marching through the sky, on unknown orders to carry out unknown tasks.

Beautiful colors and light were dancing around to the melody of thunderous applause, cracking the sky in two. Stunning. She was held entirely captive to the forces of nature, earth, sky and water, unable to make her way out of their encumbering grasp. She was entirely at the mercy of the heavens, debilitated by her human frailty. How small she was. How very, very small.

This one last thing she could do, this one act to save her sister, had been thwarted by the power and might of nature, burdening her with a unique sense of her place in the universe. She had no power, no strength. She was just a speck in the eye of the world, unseen.

She could hold on no longer. Audrey closed her eyes, and felt no more.

# CHAPTER TWENTY-EIGHT

There was a melodic beep surrounding her head. It started quietly, as if barely there, and grew louder and louder as the timeless seconds passed. A smell hit her nose, warping her senses. It was bitter and sharp, like metal and bleach.

She started to cough, a sudden and aggressive movement. She wasn't sure if it caused her lungs to ache, or just brought the pain to her attention. Her throat was on fire, an excruciating pain that rippled up her body. She tried to swallow, but her mouth was dry, like sandpaper.

A hand touched her, of that she was sure. She flinched, unprepared. She was still staring into the blackness; her heavy eyes closed. Slowly she tried to lift her eyelids. It took her longer than she was expecting. She fluttered her eyes, open then closed, open then closed, trying to find the strength to see again.

Finally, she managed to lift them enough that they stayed open. Her blurred vision took time to clear. The foggy shape sitting near her came lethargically into view.

"Audrey?" Mary's raspy voice was quiet, but Audrey heard it nevertheless. She sat in a wheelchair, cloaked in a hospital gown, to the right of Mary's bed. Her hand was on Mary's arm.

"Hey," she said, in a voice just as croaky as Mary's. "You're awake. Finally."

"What..." she took a shallow breath, "What happened?"

Audrey looked at Mary, her face portraying her deliberation. Mary's mind was too clouded; her memories scattered around. She remembered reading the will, remembered running out of the house in a fury, but any memory beyond that seemed too far away to reach.

"Just another uneventful night," Audrey said with a small, sad smile.

"Mary!" Emily gasped as she entered the room, a cafeteria coffee in hand. "You're awake! Are you okay? How are you?" She sat on the side of her bed and touched her hand to Mary's cheek. "I was so worried."

Jamie walked in behind Emily. He lingered by the door, unspeaking. The sullen look on his face was deeper and darker than usual. He stared at Mary darkly.

"She's a little groggy," Audrey rasped. "I don't think she remembers much."

"Do you, honey?" Emily asked. "Do you remember?"

Her face was earnest and too close to Mary's for her to be able to focus her tired eyes. She pressed her head back into the pillow and reading the signs, Emily backed up.

"No, I don't," Mary croaked. "What's going on? What's wrong with me? What's wrong with Audrey?"

"You tried to kill yourself." It was Jamie who spoke. His voice was acidic and cold. He stabbed his eyes at her, a black look passing across his face.

Emily looked back to Jamie, and Mary was unable to read the expression that she gave him. Jamie looked down at the floor as Emily turned back to face her daughter.

"You jumped overboard, in the middle of the lake. But it's okay, we don't have to talk about it right now."

"What? I don't understand. I don't..." Mary ravaged her mind for the memories and stumbled across them. The scenes replayed for her, and her breaths became jagged and heavy.

"Breathe," Emily cautioned. "Just breathe."

"I'm sorry," she whimpered through reigning tears. "I'm so sorry."

Emily leaned towards her daughter and hugged her close. "It's okay, honey, it's okay. You're safe now. That's what matters. Everything is going to be all right."

Mary sobbed into Emily's blouse, holding her as tightly as her weak form would allow. Emily pulled back and brushed Mary's knotted hair out of her face, wiping her tears away with her thumbs.

"You have nothing to be sorry for." She managed a smile. "Everything is fine. You're okay, you're okay."

Mary's eyes shifted to Audrey, who sat still in her chair. "What about Audrey?" she asked. "What happened to you?"

"Nothing," Audrey said, smiling feebly. "I'm fine."

"She jumped in after you," Jamie said, aggressively. "Didn't even hesitate. She swam a kilometre out to you, found you and then brought you back to shore. But, of course, she passed out halfway back, because of the exhaustion and freezing water and the storm, so Ezekiel had to go get you both and bring you back. She nearly died saving you."

"It really...it wasn't that dramatic. It's not a big deal. You're okay now; that's what matters. So, let's just focus on that."

"Really?" Mary said weakly to Audrey. "You did that? You jumped in for me?"

Audrey stared down at her hands for a long time before looking up to answer. "You would have done the same for me."

Mary shook her head. "No. I could never be as brave as you."

"No," Jamie spat. "You couldn't."

He turned from the room and left. He walked down the corridor, his heavy footfalls echoing down the halls. He scoffed loudly at the events of the evening that had almost changed everything. He could have lost both of his sisters and his father within a week of each other.

How selfish could she have been? She had tried to kill herself over losing the business to Audrey. What did it matter? Was it worth more than her life? More than the brother she claimed to love? The family that needed her?

For as long as he could remember, it had been him and Mary, sticking together through all of it, through everything that came their way. To think that she would throw it all away, in the blink of an eye. She was going to abandon him for her own selfish needs.

He unwillingly imagined her watery, bloated body washing up on the shoreline. He could see her lifeless eyes staring, unseeing, at the oppressive sky above her dead corpse. Her heart no longer beating, her mind no longer thinking.

He felt nausea roll in his stomach. He had to get out of the hospital, which smelled like sickness and death.

He needed a drink.


Jaime sat on the bar stool, a glass of bourbon, neat, between his fingers. His mind was in far off places, and the exhaustion of thinking and feeling was becoming too much to bear. He downed the glass in one gulp and swiftly ordered another.

His phone buzzed in his pocket; a text message from his mother, asking where he was. He replied to stifle her worry.

*Just gone for a walk. Needed some air.*

The last thing he would ever do is tell his mother he was at a bar. She had asked him, when he turned twenty-one and was, in her mind, in danger of becoming an alcoholic, to give up drinking. He had promised he would, but what he actually meant was that he promised to stop drinking in front of her.

There would be no good in letting her know he already was an alcoholic – apparently. These days drinking whenever you want means you're an addict and need help. But that was the thing. He didn't need help. He was perfectly satisfied letting the liquid fire rage through his veins. He didn't want to stop and saw no need.

Nobody knew he drank. Not even Mary, though he presumed she had her suspicions. She knew him better than anyone. He was what they called a functioning alcoholic, though the term made him laugh. He was a functioning alcoholic, all right – only in so much as he preferred to function with alcohol. He held his liquor well and only drank more than he could handle when he was at home, usually on a weekend when he had nothing planned the next day. He didn't party hard back in Toronto because the risks of his mother finding out were too high. He liked to think of himself as responsible.

And he drank alone. Always.

Alcoholic held such negative connotations. He just liked a drink or two. If it made his mother happier to think he didn't drink, then he would keep it that way, but he saw no reason to forbid himself one of his only pleasures in life.

His second bourbon arrived, and he drank it as quickly as he did the last. His tolerance for bourbon was strong, thus the reason it was his preferred drink. He could have more before facing inebriation. He waved to the bartender for a third.

"Just keep 'em coming," he said. "It'll be easier on us both."

After his third bourbon, he began to feel a surge of fury rise up in his throat, threatening to choke the life out of him. He couldn't get over the fact that his sister was lying in a hospital bed, his other sister recovering beside her. He was in turmoil at having nearly lost her. He felt his eyes sting with the promise of tears.

How could she do it to him? How could she do it at all, so soon after the loss of their father? Their father.

Jamie started to grind his teeth together as his fourth bourbon arrived. It was all Peter's fault. All of it. Everything.

If Peter hadn't been such a manipulative workaholic, who forced his family into lives they didn't want in order to please him, none of it would have happened. They would all be happy, and normal, but they weren't, because of him. Because of what he stood for and the man that he was.

What he was trying to do now, by forcing his family to be crammed into confined spaces for a week and manipulating them into thinking that he was a good man, was a joke. They were who they were because of him, and there was nothing that could be done about it.

Mary was unhappy. Jamie had known this for longer than anyone. She threw herself into her work so vigorously because she didn't know what else to do. Her entire life had been about getting Peter's approval because she never really, truly had it. It was as though Peter was only capable of caring about one child at a time, and even that he didn't do well. It seemed that whoever was most successful was the one he poured his time and energy into. The time and energy he had left over, anyway. And then, all of a sudden, the timer ran out and he would be completely disinterested again.

Audrey had been the favourite when they were growing up, but Peter had hardly looked at her in years. It had, if Jamie was honest, given him some pleasure to see Audrey and Peter's relationship waste away, just as his relationship with Peter had when he was younger.

For a while, it seemed as though he had Peter's approval; he had his love. It had lasted for a few months before it vanished into thin air, and he had no time for his only son again. So Jamie worked harder and harder and harder. He and Mary had been competing professionally, out of a desire for their father's attention, for years. Rarely did it ever come between them, but Jamie had deduced that the reason for that was because they relied on each other for any sense of familial belonging.

Jamie downed another drink. His thoughts were running so quickly through his mind, filtering through the drink in his blood, getting scattered and confusing.

He just wanted to stop. He wanted to stop thinking, stop feeling, stop being. He just wanted to take a break, to not have to live for just a moment, just to catch his breath. Life was a train that never stopped at any station, and he just wanted, for just a moment, a reprieve.

"Bartender!" his words were slightly slurred. "Tequila!"

The bartender walked over to him and shook his head, a mixture of pity and disgust playing with his facial features.

Jamie pointed a finger in his face. "Don't judge me. My sister just died!" Jamie figured it was close enough to the truth.

"I'm sorry, man," the bartender said, pouring him the tequila. "This one is on me, okay?"

Jamie dipped his head, dramatically, in thanks. He lifted the glass to his lips and tasted the rim. His tongue burned with the flavour. He emptied the glass into his mouth and felt the fire in his soul. After three more, he had forgotten the reason he had come there in the first place, abandoned any sense of care or concern.

The jukebox in the corner began to play *Walk This Way* by Aerosmith. It had been Jamie's favourite song in high school but he hadn't heard it in years.

"Yes!" he bellowed. "This is the one!" His words ran together in a way that he couldn't control.

Jamie got up from his seat, the toxicity of bourbon and tequila having well and truly taken him beyond the point of drunk.

"*Walk this way,*" he screeched out of time with the song.

A dozen pairs of eyes turned to face him as he bumped from table to table, flaunting his most impressive walk, to go along with the song. He sang along poorly with the lyrics, and as the chorus hit its climax, Jamie turned and jumped up on the bar.

"Get the hell down!" the bartender shouted, tugging at his jeans.

Oblivious, Jamie began to strut down the bar, squawking the chorus over and over again.

Suddenly Jamie was on his back. The bouncer had yanked him off the bar and thrown him to the ground. Jamie cackled with his perceived hilarity of the situation, still muttering along with the lyrics, as the bouncer picked him up and dropped his body outside, just a few feet away from the gutter.

Jamie's laughter gave way to sobs. Uncontrollable cries, the reason for which he was entirely unaware, poured out of his chest, bubbling out of his eyes. He rolled, and threw up in the gutter, spit and tears mixing all over his face. He lay with his face against the concrete, heavy, fat tears lumbering down his face, in front of a pile of sick.

A small hand rested on top of his back, before someone sat down beside him. "It's okay," she said. "I'm here."

Jamie didn't know who she was; his mind wasn't working anymore. He felt as though there was something familiar about the way she talked, something recognizable about her perfume, but he couldn't place her.

"Come here." She pulled him up towards her, until his head was resting on her lap. She was warm and smelled like flowers. Jamie closed his eyes and let the tears continue to fall.

# CHAPTER TWENTY-NINE

Jamie woke up to the smell of bacon and maple syrup. His head was throbbing, and his stomach sloshed with too much liquid.

He sat up with a groan, rubbing his eyes, and came face to face with a dog.

"Um..." Jamie had unwittingly entered into a staring competition with a giant bulldog. The tan and white dog glared at him like a father would at his teenage daughter's prom date. "Hi."

Jamie's head was spinning enough to make it seem as if there were two dogs watching him. He lifted his hands to his chin and cradled his head in his palms.

"Good doggy?" He posed it as more of a question than a compliment, hoping that he wasn't about to lose a patch of his jeans or a finger. "I'm gonna...I'm gonna look away now and hope that you don't lunge for my face or something, okay?"

Slowly Jamie looked away from the dog, to get an idea of his surroundings. Either he had been kidnapped by someone who had a fetish for Van Gogh paintings or he had gotten drunker than he had intended.

He was sitting on a couch, dotted with tartan pillows, in the middle of a living room. Tentatively, he stood up. Immediately, the bulldog made his way to the couch and clambered up to sit in the exact spot Jamie had just been occupying. It seemed to take the dog a considerable amount of effort to make it from the floor to the lounge. He didn't quite move his back legs quick enough, and they got stuck in the front of the couch, causing the dog to act out an awkward shuffle, finally edging his way up. He turned around in the seat and plonked down, glowering up at Jamie with self-satisfaction.

"I take it I was sitting in your seat," Jamie said. "My apologies." The dog huffed and rolled onto his back.

"Oh, you're awake."

Jamie turned to face Rose, who entered the room holding a plate of pancakes and bacon, topped with two eggs, sunny side up.

"Oh no. Not you."

"Not me? Wow. You change your mind pretty quickly, don't you? One day you're begging me to go to coffee with you, another day it's oh no, not you. Hard to please."

"No," Jamie backtracked, "that's not what I mean. It's just..." Jamie looked down at himself, prepared to gesture to his not being in his finest state, and paused. "I'm not wearing a shirt."

"No. No you're not." Jamie enjoyed the tilt of her heavy accent. "Very fine deductive skills you've got there."

"Why am I not wearing a shirt? I didn't take it off, scrunch it up and throw it at someone, did I?"

"Uh no, you didn't. But I'm guessing you've done that before. I took it off you."

"Oh, right." Jamie gave her his traditional flirtatious smile. "Now I see where this is going. Did you try to take advantage of me?" Rose threw a piece of bacon at his head. "Ow. You shouldn't play with your food."

"I took your shirt off because I didn't want you to spread your sick all over my car."

"What?" Jamie's arms dropped by his side.

"You had thrown up all over your shirt, and my car is new. But it turned out to be pointless, since you threw up on the way here anyway."

"I didn't."

"Twice."

Jamie chuckled, embarrassed. "I'm sorry."

"Yes, well, after two hours, a bottle of Windex and several pairs of gloves, I got it to the point where it doesn't smell like reconstituted bourbon anymore."

"Good. Good to know."

"So, I made you some breakfast."

Jamie looked out the window. The sun was setting on the horizon. "The sun is going down, not up."

"Yes," she sighed, exasperated. "But you are, no doubt, hungover and this is exactly what you need."

She stepped forward and shoved the plate into his hands.

"Thank you."

She crossed her arms angrily.

"You're mad," he gathered.

"Nope."

"You're angry at me."

"Not even a little."

"Definitely slightly perturbed."

"Okay," she snapped, "yes, I am. I am annoyed at you, Mr Big Shot. I found you lying face down in your own vomit in the gutter, blind from drinking. I managed to get you, stumbling, to my car, and then you threw up twice, one of which was in my lap! You grabbed my boob when I was getting you into the house, and now my living room smells like a homeless shelter."

"Hang on just a minute, I didn't ask for your help. I didn't need your help."

"Oh sure, of course you didn't need my help. You were just passed out in your own bad life decisions, in the middle of the street. I could have left you there."

"Yeah!" Jamie raised his voice. "You could have!"

"Oh, fine!" Rose shouted back. "You know, I was right about you!"

"What's that supposed to mean?"

"It means you're an arse!"

"A what? I can't understand Leprechaun."

"I'm Scottish!" Rose shouted.

Jamie picked up a piece of bacon at threw it at her. It got caught in her tight, red curls.

"Did you just throw bacon at me?" she hissed.

"You threw bacon at me first!"

Rose grabbed a fistful of pancake and squashed it against his face, holding her hand against his cheek for long enough to really rub it in.

Jamie's mouth popped open in horror. He picked up an egg and wrapped his fist around it over her head until the yolk poured through his fingers and into her hair.

Her electric green eyes illuminated in ferocity.

"That's it!" she bellowed. She turned around and ran into the kitchen, disappearing from sight.

"Running away already?" he called after her.

She stormed back into the room holding a large red mixing bowl full of pancake batter. "I never back down from a fight." She scooped up a handful of batter and flung it across his face.

An intense war of food began, starting in the living room and ending in the hallway, where Rose slipped on a puddle of egg and crashed against the floor in a fit of laughter. Jamie fell down beside her, laughing so hard that his stomach ached.

He couldn't help but notice how glorious Rose looked, her cheeks flushed from laughter, egg yolk dripping from her hair and flour dusted all over her clothes. She was like light and happiness, wrapped into one person, cascading around him like a torrent of beauty. Perhaps he was being too melodramatic. She made him feel that way, though, and he didn't feel the need to adjust his thinking.

"You are beautiful," he said, without thinking. "You know that?"

"You're still a little drunk, I think." She pawed a clump of egg white out of a ringlet and slapped it onto the ground.

"No, I mean it. Look at you."

"All right, there, Casanova," she said, standing up. "Ugh. Look at this place. Look at what you started!"

"I don't think I started it. You threw the first piece of bacon."

"Let's not get into this again. Otherwise, I'll have to show you who's boss."

"I do like a woman in charge," he said, winking.

Rose rolled her eyes. "Sure you do."

"What's that supposed to mean?"

Rose bent down and picked up the bowl of batter. "Well, all men are the same. They say they want a woman with brains, with drive. But the moment she has an opinion, you get all shocked and indignant and call her 'high maintenance'."

Jamie looked off into the distance, pensively, before returning her gaze. "I'm starting to see where you've gone south in other relationships."

"Exactly my point. You say you love a woman in charge but-"

"Oh, no, wait, now. I said like, not love. I mean, you're cute and all but I'm just not ready for that kind of commitment."

Rose licked pancake batter off of her lips, and the sight of it was unexpectedly alluring to Jamie, who subconsciously leaned towards her.

"Oh," Rose chuckled sweetly, "would you look at that."

She pulled down the front of her blouse enough to reveal the top lace of her red bra. She pressed her forefinger against the top of her left breast and drew a long line until she had collected all the batter that was there. She lifted her finger to her mouth and closed her lips around it, fluttering her eyelids.

Jamie's mouth had fallen open, and his face was just an inch or two away from hers. His eyes fluctuated from ogling her cleavage to watching her slowly pull her finger out of her mouth.

She moaned slightly and smiled coyly and parted her thick red lips invitingly. Just as Jamie was about to surrender to her intoxicating appeal, she withdrew and sighed.

"I suppose you're right about my last relationships. I really have no idea how to please a man."

As she walked into the kitchen, a satisfied smirk on her face, Jamie blew out a puff of air and bent himself in half, to alleviate sudden and unexpected pressure.

"Coming to help me clean?" Rose called.

"I'll be right there," Jamie said, breathlessly. "Just give me a minute."

# CHAPTER THIRTY

Audrey sat beside the hospital bed, the empty room feeling ominous and cold. She had been discharged twenty minutes ago, but was yet to return to her room for a change of clothes. The sun had fallen behind the hills and the night was taking up arms, preparing for yet another evening.

The events of the long night before were still fresh in her mind. She sat motionless in the dark room, staring at Mary, who was lost somewhere in deep sleep. She felt she had somehow changed.

Sitting as still as stone, watching the silent rise and fall of Mary's chest, she was, in her own mind, a different person than the woman she had been yesterday. She saw flashes of angry water trying to drown her, glimpses of moonlight breaking through heavy cloud and rain, images of Mary's unbreathing floating body. Should she have been afraid of these things? Should she feel fearful at having nearly lost her life? She wasn't sure. She only knew that she didn't feel anything at all, save for deep gratitude at Mary's continued existence.

"How are you, sweetheart?" Emily walked into the room with a plastic wrapped sandwich and a bottle of orange juice.

Audrey looked up at her mother's entrance and stood up from the chair, allowing her to take her place. "I'm fine. You?"

"Still a little shaken up. As is to be expected, I suppose. Are you going to go get changed out of that gown? I brought you a new set of clothes today."

"Yeah, I know. Thanks. I'll go now."

As Audrey turned from the room, Emily quietly called after her. "Wait. Audrey, you were amazing. Really, really amazing. Thank you. You saved her life." Emily took Audrey's hand in hers and smiled weakly. "You know, I have never been so scared in my life. I thought I was going to lose you both. Thank God for Ezekiel."

"Yeah," Audrey whispered, her heart fracturing a little at the sound of his name. "Thank God."

Audrey slowly made her way down the corridor. She was strong enough to walk now, having bid farewell to the mandatory wheelchair earlier in the day, but she was still feeling weak and sore.

Approaching her room, she wondered where Ezekiel was now. He had saved her life, but more than that he had saved Mary's as well. If it weren't for him, they would both be dead; just corpses lying in the morgue like their father had been.

She remembered him giving Mary mouth to mouth, bring her back to life, before he turned his attention to her. He had stayed with her, she recalled, her head cradled in his lap, as she came in and out of consciousness.

Then suddenly she was on an ambulance and the next time she woke up it had been in a hospital bed. Jamie had been sitting there with her, asleep on a chair, with his feet crossed at the ankles on the end of her bed.

Emily was in with Mary. They had divided and conquered.

Audrey turned into her room and jumped with fright. "Ezekiel!" she exclaimed, his presence in her room startling her. "What are you doing here?"

He sat on the chair on the far side of her room, hunched over and leaning towards the empty bed. He looked up at her as she entered, and Audrey noticed how red his eyes were.

"I'm sorry," he said, "I didn't mean to frighten you."

"No, it's...it's fine. I'm easily startled." Audrey walked forwards and started awkwardly shifting around the clothes perched on the end of her bed, tucking her underwear out of sight.

"I just thought I would come by. I wanted to see how you were. Norah said you were doing fine, but I guess I wanted to see for myself."

"Oh, right," Audrey said, picking up the clothes and hugging them to her chest. "Yeah, I am. I'm doing fine."

"Good."

A moment of uncomfortable silence passed between them as Audrey tried to figure out what her next step should be. He had killed a man. But he had saved two lives. Did that somehow equal out his wrongdoing?

"Where is Norah?" Audrey settled for asking.

"Baking. Like a madwoman. You know her, when she worries about people, she cooks for them. You're going to go home to enough food to end world hunger, I think."

Audrey chuckled, and another silence fell over the room.

"Are you going to get changed?" Zeke asked, eyeing the clothes Audrey was squeezing in her arms.

"Oh! Right. Yes. I was. I'll just be a minute."

The bathroom attached to her room was small, and she had a great deal of difficulty shifting herself from a hospital gown and into jeans and a jumper in the enclosed space.

"Are you alright?" Zeke asked as she toppled forwards and

hit her head on the closed door, letting out a shriek.

"Fine. Just fine." Audrey replied. Maybe she wasn't a different person, after all. She was still equally as awkward. But her mind was definitely quieter.

Some time later, she reappeared from the bathroom, fully clothed. "How's that?" she asked. "Better?"

"Much better," Ezekiel said. "You look like yourself again. I think a little colour is returning to your face."

Audrey smiled, unsure what to do. Her heart ached to see him sitting there, looking drawn and pale. His eyes were red and puffy, as though he had been shedding tears. Slowly, Audrey walked to his side of the room and perched herself on the end of the bed.

She looked down at her hands, clicking her nails, before she met his eyes. "Thank you, Ezekiel."

"It was nothing," Ezekiel said, sitting back in the chair as if disregarding her statement.

"No." Audrey leaned forward and took Ezekiel's face between her hands. "I wouldn't be here without you. Neither would Mary. You saved our lives. You saved my life Ezekiel, and I can't ever repay you for that. Thank you. Really and truly. Thank you."

She held his eyes for an ageless time, wet with unshed tears. The deep brown swallowed her whole, taking her home. She remembered him saying when they were walking in the woods that loving someone was as much about her as it was about the person she loved. She would have to choose how she loved them, and what she loved about them.

Would she love the shadow of Ezekiel? The way he would

live on in her memory, a perfect and unattainable man? Would she love the idea of him? Or would she love him – exactly as he was, right in that moment?

Audrey had known that a time was coming that she would have to make a choice about the person she wanted to be, but at the time she had thought it would be in relation to her father.

Sitting in a hospital room, with the man that had saved her life and touched her heart, Audrey realised it had been about Ezekiel all along. In that second, that split in time and space, Audrey made her decision.

Audrey brought Ezekiel's face to hers. Slowly she allowed her lips to brush against his, tasting his love. Tracing her tongue along his lower lip, she kissed him deeply and passionately, allowing what remained of her strong resolve to dissipate and dissolve in the hunger she felt for him.

At last they parted, anew and breathless. Ezekiel smiled, and Audrey wiped his eyes with her sleeve.

Zeke laughed and kissed her forehead. "So," he said, "how about a lift home?"

# CHAPTER THIRTY-ONE

Sitting in the front seat of his car, Audrey felt at last as though a hole in her chest had been filled.

But there was one thing she still needed to know. "Tell me," she said.

"Tell you what?" he asked.

"About the man you killed. I'm sorry for the way I acted before. It just took me by surprise. But I want you to know that this time, I'll listen. You said you could explain, and I'm ready and willing to listen."

Ezekiel looked at her warily. "You won't run away?"

"I won't run away. Literally or figuratively. We're in a moving vehicle, and I don't feel like going back to the hospital."

Ezekiel chuckled and nodded. "Okay. Here it goes. Back in Madrid, there is a group of men that call themselves the la Escorpión Blanco – the White Scorpions. They run drugs and guns, launder money, work in kidnapping and murder for hire. Their leader, Aurelio Barrero, killed my son."

"Your son?" Audrey raised a hand to her mouth in both shock and horror.

"Yes. He was not my biological son, but that did not make him any less my son. My best friend Diego married his high school sweetheart, Elena. They died in a car accident when Teodoro was just a few months old. They named me his guardian in their will, and I adopted him as my own."

"Oh, Ezekiel, I'm so, so sorry. I can't even imagine." Audrey squeezed his knee, a small gesture, the only one she could think to carry out.

Zeke didn't speak for a long while. A heavy hush filled the car, bitter and weighty. When he finally spoke again, Audrey could sense the sorrow in his voice.

"Diego was in deep with the Scorpions. He stole something from them. I never knew until they took Teodoro. When they realised that I didn't know what he had stolen, let alone where he had hidden it, he killed Teodoro out of spite, right in front of my eyes."

"Why would they wait four years to come after you?" Audrey asked.

"Barrero was in prison for that time. As soon as he got out, they came for me."

"So, what did you do after they killed Teodoro?"

"They started coming for me. I ran as fast as I could, but Barrero caught up to me. He lunged at me, and we fought. He had a knife. I have a long scar down my leg from where he cut me. Somehow I managed to get the knife from him and I don't know what happened. One minute I was fighting for my life, the next I was standing over Barrero's body, his own knife in his chest. I stitched myself up at home, and I got on a plane and came here. The timing was good, as my father was sick. I have been hiding from the Scorpions ever since."

Audrey felt ashamed. She had refused to listen to his explanation, denied any possibility that he was a good man. Things were not always black and white, and it was a lesson that Audrey had not yet mastered.

"I'm so sorry, Ezekiel," Audrey whispered. "I should have known. I'm sorry."

"It's all right," Ezekiel replied. "I understand. Your reaction was perfectly justified. I'm just glad you gave me a second chance."

"I don't think I ever had a choice."

"What do you mean?" Ezekiel asked as he pulled into Norah's property.

"I think I was always yours." Audrey smiled as he met her eyes. She leaned over and fell into his embrace.

She was right where she wanted to be. More than that, she was exactly who she wanted to be.

# Chapter Thirty-Two

Jamie finally replied to the dozens of text messages his mother had sent him. *I'm fine. Stop worrying. I'll be back at Aunt Norah's soon.*

"You know," he said, slipping his phone back into his pocket, "technically you kidnapped me."

Rose washed the final dish and handed it to Jamie, who had a checked tea towel slung over his shoulder. "Oh, really? And how do you figure that?"

"Well," Jamie said, taking the bowl and wiping it dry, "you took me back here, to Canim Lake. I was an hour's drive away from here, and you picked me up, put me in your car and drove me back to your lair."

"My lair? I like that. Makes me feel like a super villain."

"Oh, you are. You are a super villain. You have kidnapped a famous photographer. I'm surprised the police aren't breaking in through your windows right now."

"Hmm," she sighed, drying her hands. "I guess you're not as important as you think you are."

Jamie smiled. "I guess not." Her green eyes flashed with mischief as he watched her, entirely under her spell. "But you know, if you wanted to invite me back to your place there were simpler ways."

"You got me. I just wanted to have you all to myself."

"I thought as much. So, now that you have me, what are you going to do with me?"

"I could kill you and sell your organs on the black market."

"Mmm," Jamie shook his head. "That's been done too many times."

Rose put a finger to her chin and feigned deep thought. "I could make you my personal slave."

"You could, I suppose." Jamie stepped closer to her until his body was touching hers. He bent his head down and whispered. "But I think there are better uses for me."

"You're right," she said. "There are. Follow me."

Rose turned from the kitchen and walked into the living room. She gestured for him to take a seat, and then she sat down on the floor in front of him.

"Come on," she snipped, when Jamie remained unmoving.

"What do you want me to do?" he laughed.

"I have a knot in my shoulders that I just can't get out. You can massage me."

Jamie's mouth popped open. "Well played, my young Padawan."

Rose smiled as Jamie's fingers wrapped around her shoulders.

"You know," Jamie said after some time, "you're kind of amazing. You do see that, right?"

"Oh, every time I look in the mirror."

"I mean it." Jamie traced his fingers along her neck and watched her shiver involuntarily. "You surprise me. Not a lot of people can do that. Although, my father just blew me away a little."

"Your father?"

"Yeah, he died. Just, I don't know, a week ago. I lose track of time up here. That's why we're here. It's some twisted idea of him getting our family back together again. He wanted us to be closer. I didn't think it would work, but, you know, I actually do feel closer to them. Or I did, until Mary tried to kill herself last night."

Rose turned around, her eyes wide. "What are you talking about?"

"I had just come out of the hospital, where Mary and Audrey, my sisters, were. Mary jumped out of a row boat, and Audrey was like some crazed superhero. She didn't even pause for a second. She ran down the pier and threw herself into the water and swam after her. But Mary had rowed out so far, and the water was so cold, that Audrey nearly died trying to save her. My Aunt Norah's friend saved them. It was messed up."

"Why?" Rose asked. "Why would she want to kill herself?"

"My father left the business to Audrey. She is this unsuccessful, money hating artist who lives in this crappy apartment in the city. Funny thing though – she's happy. But here's the kicker – she's not even his kid. We just found out my Mom had an affair, and it led to Audrey. She's never shown the slightest interest in the business. I guess when Dad left it to her, Mary kind of saw it like some giant screw you from him and thought, sure, I'll kill myself."

"It would have been more than that," Rose objected. "I'm sure it would have been something deeper than just a business being left to someone else."

"The business is worth billions."

"Even so," Rose said. "You should talk to her."

"Yeah," Jamie said. "Maybe."

"I'm really sorry." Rose got up on her knees, so she was eye to eye with him. "I'm really, really sorry." Jamie didn't move or say a word. He felt nauseated at being so close to her, a good kind of nauseated.

He could not come to terms with her beauty; it radiated out of her. It was more than her face. Her beauty came from much deeper than that.

To win her heart, he knew he was going to have to change. He would have to say goodbye to his lifestyle, goodbye to partying and women. He would have to stop drinking. He couldn't be with someone like Rose when he was intoxicated every evening. He felt a twinge of horror at the thought of giving up the booze, and irrational anger at Rose filled his chest.

Why should he have to give up drinking for her? If she didn't like him the way he was, that was her problem. He wanted to stand up, to burst out the doors and get as far away from her as possible.

Just as he was about to stand, something unexpected stopped him.

Rose kissed him. Gently and sweetly, she touched her lips to his. She tasted like rain.

Jamie was too taken aback to return the kiss. When Rose pulled back, she had a smile, so honest and raw across her face, that he could do nothing but open his mouth and tell her his deepest, darkest secret. "Rose, I think I have a drinking problem."

# CHAPTER THIRTY-THREE

Mary sat in the living room, a blanket wrapped around her shoulders and a cup of hot coffee in her hands. She was staring out the window, her gaze was unwavering.

Audrey walked in and sat down beside her. "Hey," she said quietly.

"Hi," Mary said, looking away from the window for the first time all morning.

"How are you?" Audrey asked.

Mary bit her lower lip. "I'm fine. How are you?"

"I'm good." Audrey smiled at her and tucked her stringy hair behind her ear. "Hey, you got room in there for two?"

"Sure." Mary opened the blanket and Audrey settled herself in beside her, tugging the blanket over her shoulder. "Um, I don't know what to say, but I just...I just...I want you to know that...it wasn't because of you...the business." Mary's convoluted sentence was frustrating her. She shook her head to clear her scattered thoughts. "It wasn't because he left you the business that I...you know...jumped. Thank you. Thank you for saving me. It was so incredibly brave of you."

"I love you, Mary."

Mary swallowed hard, squashing her discomfort with emotions. "I love you, too, Audrey."

Devoid of any fear, Audrey looped her arms around Mary's waist and snuggled into her side. Mary, filled with fresh love for her sister, rested her head on Audrey's.

"This is quite the picture," Jamie said as he entered the room.

"Where have you been?" Emily asked, entering the room. "You told me last night that you would be home soon. In case you hadn't noticed, it's a new day!"

"Mom, I'm sorry. I was with someone."

"The girl?" Audrey asked. "The...what's her name? Rose!"

"Yes, I was with Rose. But not like that. Nothing happened. Well, not nothing. She kissed me."

Mary smiled. "That's great, Jamie."

"Also, she's coming to stay with me in Toronto for a while."

"What?" Emily exclaimed. "Don't you think you're moving too quickly?"

"It's not like that, Mom. Not yet, anyway. She's going to..." he paused, shame and fear pounding against the cage of his mind. "She's going to be my sponsor."

"Your sponsor?" Emily asked. "For what?"

"Mom." Jamie took her hands in his and stared deeply into her eyes. "I'm an alcoholic. I'm so sorry. I've let you down. All of you. And I lied to you, Mom. Please forgive me. I'm all set – I'll be checking into rehab when I get home. I don't want you to worry."

Emily held Jamie close to her, hugging him tighter than she ever had before. "Oh, Jamie. I knew. I knew all along. I was waiting for you to be ready. I'm so proud of you."

Jamie buried his head into Emily's neck and wept.

"Oh good!" Norah said, "You're all here!" Norah walked into the living room with two serving trays of pastries and pies. "I cooked! That's what you all need, after staying at the hospital and being subjected to their food. If you can even call it food." She placed the tray down as Emily and Jamie parted. "Eat up!

It's just what the doctor ordered after all you lot have been through."

Jamie laughed and wiped his face, before snatching up a muffin and a slice of pie. Both hands full of food, he took alternating bites until his hands were empty. Then, he returned for a refill.

As he was about to take a bite out of an apple Danish, he paused, and passed it to Mary. She looked up at her brother, eyes wide, and took the Danish with trembling hands.

"I know it was more," he said. "I know it was more. And I'm here. We're all here."

"Thank you," Mary whimpered.

"Right," he said, "now that that's out of the way. Here is to the hero of the hour. Or the decade, really." He dropped down beside Audrey and slapped a hand against her knee. "Thanks, sis. You're incredible."

With a light heart, Audrey bit into a Danish.

# CHAPTER THIRTY-FOUR

The sun was setting over the trees on the far horizon, splattering red, purple and orange across the canvas of the sky. The unseasonable warmth of the breeze had stilled until there was not a sound around them. It was tranquil and pure, like the scene of a poem.

The day had been sweet, and the moment in which they had found themselves contrasted deeply.

The black-clad figures, which made up the Wood family, were immobile as they stood at the end of the pier, preparing to find a way to voice a final farewell somehow. A farewell that seemed impossible. Emily stood in the centre, a flowing black dress and matching cardigan keeping her frame.

She held the maroon urn, embossed with Peter David Wood, in her hands. Its weight seemed extraordinary in her hands. A lifetime of memories and a love that had penetrated her soul trampled and burned into a small jar that could fit into her hands. There was a feeling so terrible in her stomach; she felt she wanted to throw the urn and run, as far away as she could. To leave this horrible moment and never look back.

How could she say goodbye? She couldn't. She refused. Peter was as much a part of her as her own heart. The idea of saying goodbye to him, of letting go of the man she had loved more than anyone, for most of her life, was a task too weighty for her to undertake.

She still felt him with her. Right beside her, like he never left. She could still smell his cologne, hear his footsteps. Emily dropped to her knees, unable to support herself any longer, as the weight of anguish lay too heavy a burden on her shoulders. She wrapped her arms around her waist, holding the urn close to her heart and sobbed. She let out a sorrowful cry, overwhelmed by the madness of a grief so real she thought it would – should – stop her heart, right in that moment. For what was the point in carrying on in a world in which Peter did not exist?

What a fool she had been, losing all of those years. Countless priceless moments that she could cherish for all of her days were sacrificed because of her pride. The tears fell freely, aggressively, as she tried to purge herself of the guilt and heartache. She feared, however, that it would be an affliction she would forever carry until her own ashes were to be scattered, right here in this place, to re-join her husband in death as she should have in life.

The sobs rose up her throat, choking her until she couldn't breathe. She didn't know how she was supposed to go on, what she was supposed to do from here. Sorrow burned through her veins like a blazing fire that would never go out, ripping through her weak body with the intention to slaughter her.

Audrey dropped to her mother's side and pressed herself against her, wrapping her arms around her shoulders. She could do nothing to mask the pain; she could only be there and feel the loss. There was a distinct feeling that something was missing, that a giant hole had been carved into the soul of the family; irreparable and gruesome, a festering wound. Audrey believed it would never be healed, they would only continue to learn how to deal with it, how to bear the melancholy each day. Mary and Jamie joined their mother, letting their legs dangle over the edge. Norah stood behind them, a pillar of strength and determination. She kept them under her care and watch, like a mother eagle with her young.

Emily's sobs gave way to silent tears that refused to cease. She squeezed harder against the urn, trying to feel her husband's strong grasp around her body. She looked out over the water, seeing him in her mind's eye, proposing to her on the boat in the middle of the lake. She saw him bend down on one knee, watched the tears form in his eyes. She recalled the feeling of completeness wash over her in that moment, knowing that she would never again have to be alone. Knowing that someone loved her, completely and fully, and that nothing could ever take that away from her.

Knowing that she belonged.

Finally, she was home and whole. Her throat closed as she saw herself leap into his arms, wobbling the boat. His warm embrace enveloped her, and he whispered in her ears words that she would never forget.

"I am yours and you are mine. From this day on. I love you, and I will never leave you."

"You lied!" Emily shouted into the empty air that carried the memory. "You lied!" She fought against the lump in her throat to voice the words that erupted out of the wreckage of her heart. He had promised he would never leave her, a promise he had made when he had no control. He had promised.

"You said..." she choked on violent sobs, "you said you'd never leave me! You swore it."

The boat disappeared and the man in her memories, which played out before her, stood still and silent on the water's surface. He was the Peter she had loved for all of those years. The man who had told her she was the only good thing about him. The man who would sacrifice it all for her. The man who had captured her heart. The sobs rose as she saw him raise a hand in farewell, saying his last goodbye to his only love, before he disappeared from the cinema of her mind.

Audrey looked out to the water, tears rolling uncontrollably down her face, wondering what it was that her mother could see. She held her tightly until her cries became soundless. Withdrawing from the embrace, Audrey wiped her tears away with her sleeves, looking to Mary and Jamie. They looked back at her, faces red and wet from mourning. Mary stretched out a hand to Audrey, a softness in her eyes that she had never seen before. She gripped Mary's hand and squeezed, making up for years of lost time, abandoned closeness.

"I love you," Mary mouthed through tears to the woman she was only just beginning to treat as her sister.

Wet teardrops fell from Audrey's eyes and she squeezed Mary's hand all the more. "I love you," she returned.

Emily slowly lifted the lid of the urn and passed it to Jamie, who took it with shaking hands. She removed a handful of all that remained of her love and scattered it across the lake. The ashes fell onto the surface of the water, causing minute ripples to stretch across the mirrored glassy lake.

Mary, his first, withdrew a handful and held it up. "I miss you, Daddy," she whispered inaudibly, before gently tossing the ashes into the water.

Jamie, his son, cupped the ashes in his palms, soft cries shaking his jaws. He let the ashes fall with his eyes tightly closed.

Audrey, his Mona Lisa, let the memories of her father swallow her heart as she allowed his ashes to trickle through her fingers like sand.

Peter was finally where he was supposed to be. At home, with his family.

# Chapter Thirty-Five

Audrey couldn't sleep. She had been staring at the roof, under the protection of her blankets, for at least an hour. She had seen the sun rise through the gap in her curtain.

There was too much to think about for her to sleep. She had no idea what she was supposed to do.

Finally, an avenue of her life was going well – she and Ezekiel were falling in love.

But what was going to happen when she had to leave? Emily had decided they would stay a few days longer so that both she and Mary could regain their full strength. But they were due to head off in three days. What would happen to her relationship with Ezekiel?

Audrey sat up and threw the covers off of her body. She dressed quickly in old torn jeans, a striped sweater and a dark scarf. She withdrew her knee high boots and tucked her jeans into them.

She opened her door quietly and tip-toed down the hall. She stepped over the third plank of wood to the left, three feet away from Mary's room. From experience, she knew it let out a horrid creak.

Quietly, she descended the staircase and crossed the floor to the front door. Outside, it was warmer than she had been expecting. It would rain heavy come evening time.

Audrey made her way for the line of trees, her mind mulling over thought after thought. The sound of her boots squelching into the ground and the early morning chirp of birds was the only sound. The house disappeared from view as she waded deeper and deeper into the trees.

What was she supposed to do? Her father – who wasn't even her father – had left her a business worth billions. She had never had a desire to be in business. She had just wanted to paint.

She stopped at the log on which she had rested before, but she couldn't sit. She was too agitated. She shifted her weight back and forth, from her right foot to her left. A few short weeks ago, when everything was normal, and her father was still alive, she had thought that nothing could ever change her opinion on the family business, Wood Incorporated. She barely even knew what the business did. She knew it had something to do with acquiring other businesses and building and selling them, or something of the sort, but she didn't know the first thing about it.

However, everything was different now. Her father had given it to her. Out of Emily, Mary and Jamie, he had chosen to give the business to Audrey.

Was it just some sort of guilt inspired act which he didn't really mean? Was he losing his mind? Was he trying to make amends?

Audrey tried to clear her mind.

She pulled out the letter and read it again. She had lost count of how many times she had read it the night before. After scattering the ashes, they had all had a quiet family dinner and disappeared into their own corners of the world to deal with their loss in whatever way they could. Audrey had tried to find solace in the last words he spoke to her, but she found only more confusion. What did he want from her?

Reading it this time, however, and standing out in the fresh air with the powder blue sky hovering above her, it seemed to make more sense. Maybe her father wasn't finished bringing them all back together yet. Or maybe he wanted to ensure they would never drift apart again.

He had said that the business was hers to do with as she wished.

She finally realised what her father wanted. She knew what she was going to do.

Audrey's head snapped to the right. The pungent smell of smoke hit her hard in the face. Without thinking twice, Audrey sprinted towards the cottage and the people she knew were inside.

She pushed her legs harder and harder as she sprinted through the trees, desperate to make it home.

Her passage through the woods seemed to extend the harder she ran. She felt she was never going to make it.

Finally, she burst through the line and out into the open. The cabin was on fire.

She paused for the briefest second to take in the image before her. Giant orange flames engulfed the house, licking at the wood and dissolving anything in its path.

"Ezekiel!" she screamed at the top of her lungs. "Ezekiel! Help!"

Four men stood in front of the house, red cans of gasoline in their hands. They were laughing, gleeful at their efforts.

Audrey ran forward, fear crippling her body. She pushed through the feeling that her limbs were dead weights and ran towards the cabin. "Ezekiel!"

Ezekiel emerged from the cabin; a crowbar raised above his head. He saw the men who he immediately recognised, and watched in horror as Audrey ran towards them.

"No!" he shouted. "Audrey, stay back!"

The sound of his voice caught their attention. The men turned and saw Ezekiel. They looked at the house, then back to the cottage and realised their mistake. La Escorpión Blanco had found him, and it was finally time for their revenge.

Abandoning the cabin, the men darted towards Ezekiel, who ran back into his cottage, returning seconds later with a gun laced between his fingers.

# Chapter Thirty-Six

Audrey saw the men chase after Ezekiel and watched him run back inside. There was nothing she could do for him while her family was trapped inside the cabin.

Audrey pushed open the front door, now unguarded, and immediately covered her mouth. Black smoke was everywhere.

"Mom!" she shouted. "Mary!"

Audrey swam through the smoke, past the living room that was engulfed in flames. She made her way up the stairs slowly, in case their structure had been compromised. Down the hall, she bashed her fist against doors, trying to alert everyone around her.

"Fire!" she shouted. "Get out! Get out!"

She opened her mother's door first. She was backing away from the far wall, the outside of which was swallowed in flames, fire leaking into the room.

"Mom!" she shouted. "Get out! Go downstairs! Call for help!"

Emily retrieved her handbag, which held her cell phone, and ran downstairs to call for a fire truck.

Audrey made her way through the hall, shouting out, 'Fire!' over and over and over. Jamie popped out of his room, the smell of smoke heavy in the air.

"Help me!" she shouted.

Jamie ran to Norah's room and Audrey to Mary's. She opened the door and called for her sister, who was trapped in the room, cut off by aggressive flames.

"Mary! It's okay! I'm here." Audrey scanned the room; there

was a small pathway that Mary could use to get to freedom. Audrey stepped forward with cautious footwork. She pushed bedside table out of the way, into the line of fire and slipped behind it. She extended a hand to Mary, who was curled on the ground. Mary took her hand and followed her out of the room.

"Jamie!" she shouted.

"Here," he called back, with Norah in tow.

"Get downstairs and outside," Audrey ordered. "But there are men outside. They did this. Be careful." As her family filed past her, she stopped Jamie. "They're after Ezekiel. Help him."

Jamie nodded and dashed down the stairs. Audrey began to follow. The smoke was heavy, blinding.

She could barely breathe.

She missed a step as she descended the stairs and fell the rest of the way. She heard something crack as she landed and realised it must have been her wrist. She screamed out in pain as agony rippled through her. She had hit her head, and her vision was blurred, complicating her sight even more.

She picked herself up and made her way to the door, though something made her pause. She looked to the living room and saw what remained of her father's ashes sitting on the mantle. He had been burned once. She couldn't let him be burned again.

She pushed her way past toppled objects, aflame. The living room was swallowed in fire, but she forced herself through. Devising a path she made it to the mantelpiece, just in time to hear a loud moan. She looked up and saw the roof had cracked and was about to fall right down on top of her.

Ezekiel raised his weapon at the men coming towards him.

Two of them stopped, and another two pulled out guns of their own.

"We found you, Ezekiel," one of the men spat. Tattoo ink covered most of his body, and his face was scarred. "Just give up. You're going to die here."

"Don't take another step!" Ezekiel demanded. "Don't move!"

"Wait," a voice called. Ezekiel turned to follow the voice. A man had stepped out of their car. He was tall and broad. Ezekiel couldn't see his face clearly, but the men who were approaching him stopped where they were.

The man neared Ezekiel with each step he took, and he finally came into view. "Barrero?" Ezekiel cried. "You're...alive. How are you alive?"

"You thought you got the better of me?" Barrero chuckled. "Nobody can kill me."

Ezekiel raised his weapon higher, aiming directly for the centre of his head. Out of the corner of his eye, he saw Norah, Jamie, and Mary pour out of the house.

Where was Audrey?

"If you have killed her," Ezekiel said, "I will make you pay. There is no way you will take two people from me and live to talk about it."

"Oh, there is a *her*?" Barrero chuckled. "What's her name?"

Ezekiel refused to answer. He saw Jamie crouch and run towards the car. What was he doing?

"Come on. You can tell me. You and I, we share a special bond. I don't even want to kill you, you know? I want to turn you. I want you to work for me."

"What?" one of the men asked. "Boss, I thought we came

here to kill him."

Without looking behind him, Barrero pulled out his gun and shot the man down. "We have an opening. Are you interested? You can take Diego's place. I had a lot of trouble finding you, and you did manage to stab me. I need someone like you. Someone with guts."

Ezekiel's eyes caught something that made him smirk. "Then you should really look behind you."

The sound of a revving engine forced Barrero to turn around, just in time to see Jamie slide their own vehicle into them, knocking them all to the ground, pinning two of them under.

Ezekiel stepped up to the fallen body of Aurelio Barrero and kept the gun aimed squarely at his head. "You will never touch someone I love again."

The whirring of sirens preceded the arrival of three ambulances, two police cars and two fire trucks. As Barrero and his men were taken away, Ezekiel turned his attention to the house the firefighters were dousing with water.

Had Audrey come out? Where was she?

Norah, Emily and Mary were talking to the police, and Jamie was watching the fire go out. Audrey was nowhere to be seen.

"Audrey!" Ezekiel shouted. "Audrey!" He made it to Jamie's side in seconds. "Jamie, where is she? Where is Audrey?"

"She made it out. Hasn't she?" Jamie looked around. "She was right behind me. She was right behind me!"

Ezekiel ran to the front door, the structure of the building crumbling before his eyes. "Audrey!" he shouted. He hadn't seen her come out, and neither had Jamie. Where was she? "Audrey!"

He was going to have to go in. She had to be alive; she couldn't be dead. She had run into a burning building to save her family. She couldn't die for that. The universe wasn't that cruel.

He stepped forward, ready to go in, but was halted by somebody shouting his name. He spun around and saw Audrey walking towards him, a blanket draped over her shoulder; her wrist bandaged.

"Zeke, I'm here," she called. Her voice was weak; he could only just make it out over the cacophony of sounds around him.

"Audrey," he breathed, jogging towards her. Upon reaching her, he swept her up in his arms, spinning her around. "You're okay. You're alive."

"I'm alive," she said, hiding her face in his neck. "I'm okay. I had to save the urn."

Dropping her down onto the ground, Zeke crushed his lips against hers, unwilling to let her go. Passion and fervour combined until their kiss exploded as their lips moved in time.

Pulling back, breathless and weak, Ezekiel pressed his forehead against hers. "It's over. It's finally over."

Another police car arrived on the scene, a van, capable of carting each of the men away.

As he watched the van, which had imprisoned his past, drive away, he squeezed Audrey tightly. "I'm free."

# EPILOGUE

Audrey waited at the café for Jamie and Mary to arrive. It had been six months since they had tripped out of a burning building, barely making it out with their lives. So much had changed; everything was different now.

Rose had moved to Toronto to be Jamie's sponsor, and he had been sober for six months and four days. He had spent four weeks in rehab and quit the modelling industry. He and Rose were in a steady relationship, and working together, she as a travel writer and he as her accompanying photographer. Audrey had never seen him so well. His generally sour demeanour had been replaced; he was almost unrecognisable.

Mary had stepped back from her role at Wood and Snow, taking on fewer cases. She was leaving for Europe in two weeks. She and Audrey had never been closer. They were friends now, not just sisters.

Norah and Audrey lived together in the house just outside the city. Insurance had covered the damages to the cottage, and it was slowly being rebuilt.

"They're going to be late," Audrey muttered.

"Don't worry. They're always late." Ezekiel wrapped his broad hand around her knee. "I'm not worried."

Audrey turned to the man she loved and smiled a broad, honest smile. Her loose hair was swept to one side, lightened from her recent trip to the hairdresser. She wore new jeans and a black blouse, with a long pink coat. She had a new appreciation for herself, a sudden idea that maybe she was worth something more than she had imagined.

"You are so beautiful," Zeke said, leaning forward and kissing her forehead.

"Ew, get a room," Jamie said, as he walked in with Mary.

His long hair was cut short, cropped and neat, and his indie outfit had been passed over for loose fitting jeans and a long-sleeved black button up shirt. He sat down and winked at Zeke.

"Sorry, we're late," Mary said. "I got stuck on this one chapter and didn't pick Jamie up on time."

"How is the book coming along?" Ezekiel asked.

"Oh, great. It's so much fun." Mary's hair was growing out. She had tied it back out of her face; it was no longer jet black, but a light brown. She wore jeans and a t-shirt with a leather jacket, flat sandals and almost no make-up.

"I'm so glad," Zeke said, taking a sip of his coffee.

"Did you hear?" Audrey said. "She named her main character after me." Audrey grinned as she spun the diamond ring on the fourth finger of her left hand.

Mary rolled her eyes and ordered a coffee as the waitress arrived. "I think I owed you that. At the very least."

Audrey smiled at her sister and felt a sudden warm glow grip her heart. She hadn't realised what she was missing all these years, devoid of a real family relationship. Her world had been turned upside down, but for the better. She had decided what to do with the business. Her father had said that Wood Incorporated was hers to do with as she pleased. She finally had seen the wisdom in her father's actions as he fought to rectify the mistakes he had made that had rippled throughout the lives of his family. He had wanted to bring his family back together with the holiday in Canim Lake, but he had wanted to ensure they would never drift apart by leaving Audrey with the business.

Somewhere, deep in her heart, Audrey believed her Dad knew what she was going to do with the business, and that was why he trusted her with it. She had split the company between the three of them, ensuring that she, Mary and Jamie were all figureheads at Wood Incorporated. Through the business, their father could take care of them, even in death. Without having to have any active role in the company, save for when they wanted to, their financial future was secure, and they were each bound together by something their father had created.

"Do you have to get back to the gallery at any time?" Jamie asked.

"Nope," Audrey shook her head and smiled. "What's the point in owning your own art gallery if you can't pick and choose your hours?" Audrey smiled, her mind silent and her heart light, aware that three siblings, who had once been strangers, had been united by their father, who had found a way to be a Dad.

# THE END

# About the Author

Paige Bloomfield is a screenwriter, novelist and children's book author. She lives in Queensland, Australia, with her family and is passionate about puppies, chai lattes and squirrels. She considers Canada her second home, and spends as much time as possible there travelling and visting her friends and extended family.

# Other Books by This Author

## *Chrildren's*
### Little Sushi Roll
### Fizzy Fish

## *Fiction*
### In Case of Rain
### The Paper Heart of Jack Leatherby
### Czech Mate
### Six Degrees

*To learn more about this author or contact her, visit*
*www.hardthouse.com*